MONSTER MAYHEM

Adapted by Steve Korté
Based on the screenplay *Monster Mayhem* written by Heath Corson
Batman created by Bob Kane with Bill Finger

SIMON SPOTLIGHT
New York   London   Toronto   Sydney   New Delhi

SIMON SPOTLIGHT
An imprint of Simon & Schuster Children's Publishing Division
1230 Avenue of the Americas, New York, New York 10020
This Simon Spotlight hardcover edition December 2016
All rights reserved, including the right of reproduction in whole or in part in any form.
SIMON SPOTLIGHT and colophon are registered trademarks of Simon & Schuster, Inc.
For information about special discounts for bulk purchases, please contact Simon & Schuster
Special Sales at 1-866-506-1949 or business@simonandschuster.com.
Designed by Nicholas Sciacca
The text of this book was set in Core Sans.
Manufactured in the United States of America 1116 FFG
10 9 8 7 6 5 4 3 2 1
ISBN 978-1-4814-8007-9 (hc)
ISBN 978-1-4814-8006-2 (pbk)
ISBN 978-1-4814-8008-6 (eBook)

CHAPTER 1

On the outskirts of Gotham City, high atop a hill, stood the dark and foreboding institution known as Arkham Asylum. It took a special type of criminal to end up at Arkham. Within the asylum's walls were some of the most dangerous foes ever to fight Batman, villains who were too dangerous and sometimes too insane to be held in regular prisons.

It was Halloween night, and the stillness surrounding Arkham was abruptly disrupted by a loud crash.

BLAM!

It was the sound of a giant fist crashing through a

wall of the asylum building! Bricks fell to the ground as Solomon Grundy used the sheer force of his body to smash the rest of the way through, creating a huge, jagged hole in the side of the building.

Standing seven feet tall and weighing 517 pounds, the zombielike Grundy had been one of Batman's strongest and most dangerous enemies, and now the asylum's exterior wall was the only thing that separated him from the innocent people celebrating Halloween in nearby Gotham City. And he wasn't alone.

"Come on!" he yelled behind him as he ran toward the concrete wall that stood between him and the outside world.

"Hold up, Grundy," called a female voice. "I'm coming."

The sorceress Silver Banshee stepped through the hole, her long white hair whipping in the wind and her dead eyes blinking in the moonlight. Silver Banshee possessed superhuman strength and the power to create a sonic boom just by using her voice. As soon as she was free from Arkham, she was going to seek revenge against the heroes who had imprisoned her.

She caught up to Grundy, who was already pounding his massive fist against the concrete wall. He quickly knocked a gaping hole in it, and the two villains stepped through. Solomon Grundy and Silver Banshee quickly disappeared into the woods before anyone even knew they had escaped.

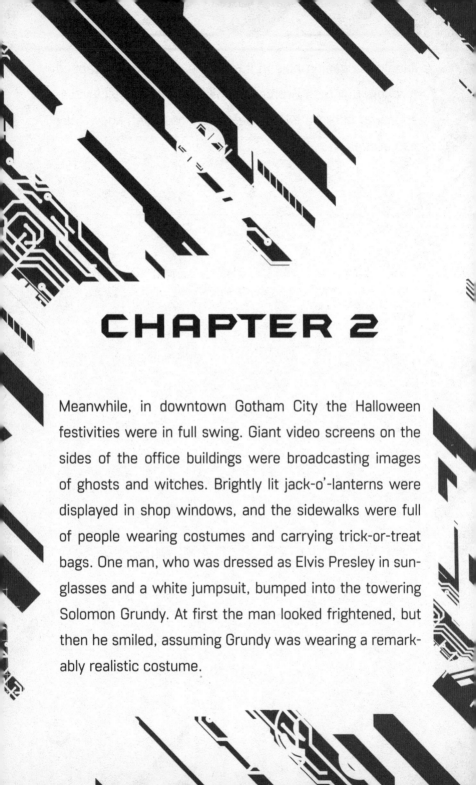

CHAPTER 2

Meanwhile, in downtown Gotham City the Halloween festivities were in full swing. Giant video screens on the sides of the office buildings were broadcasting images of ghosts and witches. Brightly lit jack-o'-lanterns were displayed in shop windows, and the sidewalks were full of people wearing costumes and carrying trick-or-treat bags. One man, who was dressed as Elvis Presley in sunglasses and a white jumpsuit, bumped into the towering Solomon Grundy. At first the man looked frightened, but then he smiled, assuming Grundy was wearing a remarkably realistic costume.

"Zombie wrestler! Nice one!" the Elvis guessed. Then he high-fived Grundy's giant hand.

As the man walked away, Grundy smiled and turned to Silver Banshee. "Grundy love Halloween!" he said.

BEEP! BEEP!

A red convertible had stopped in front of Grundy and Silver Banshee, who were standing in the middle of the street, and the driver was honking the car's horn. The driver was wearing a Batman costume, and the other two passengers were dressed as Green Arrow and Robin.

"Keep it moving, freak show!" yelled the driver.

Silver Banshee glared at the car and said, "Freak show, is it?"

The driver stood up in the car and yelled, "I *said* get out of the street!"

"Well, I hate your hero costumes, and so does my friend," said Silver Banshee.

"Lady, I don't care what you or your—" the driver started to say.

Just then Grundy reached over and easily lifted the car with one hand.

"Ah!" cried the three costumed men as Grundy shook the car and dumped the trio onto the street.

Moments later Silver Banshee was at the wheel of the convertible, cackling with glee as she and Grundy drove off.

"Faster! Go faster!" yelled Grundy with a big smile on his face.

"Coming up," said Silver Banshee, and she stepped on the gas pedal. They were soon speeding through the streets of Gotham City, weaving recklessly around other cars.

Just then a pair of flying police cars whipped around the corner, in hot pursuit of the stolen convertible. Sirens filled the air as the police vehicles flew closer.

"Policemen!" said Grundy.

"I got this," said Silver Banshee as she turned around to glare at the police cars. "Take the wheel, Grundy."

As Grundy grabbed the steering wheel, Silver Banshee hopped into the backseat of the car. Then she opened her mouth and yelled.

The explosive sonic boom of her scream slammed into one of the police cars and sent it spinning through the air and crashing to the ground.

Silver Banshee was panting heavily, trying to catch her breath.

"Why you stop?" asked Grundy.

"I have to catch my breath at some point!" Silver Banshee said angrily.

"Pull over!" came the voice of a policeman over a loudspeaker. "Pull over and give yourself up!"

"Not likely!" said Silver Banshee. Then she drew in her breath and screamed again.

Her voice hit the other police car like a sledgehammer and sent it careening through the air until it smashed into a building.

"Yessss!" yelled Grundy as he raised both of his arms in victory.

"Keep your hands on the wheel, Grundy!" said Silver Banshee.

As the villains sped through downtown Gotham City, a tall figure emerged from the shadows atop a nearby building and watched their progress. It was Nightwing, the skilled crime fighter and one of Batman's closest allies. Nightwing was Dick Grayson and had once been Batman's young partner, Robin. Now Nightwing patrolled Gotham City every night. He tapped a button on the side of his mask, which allowed the cameras within his eyepieces to zoom in on Grundy and Silver Banshee.

Nightwing didn't even turn around when he heard the soft thud of someone landing on the rooftop behind him.

"I'm glad you're here," Nightwing said, thinking Batman had arrived.

"People usually are," said a voice in response.

Nightwing spun around and saw his friend Green Arrow step into the light. Green Arrow was a super hero and an expert archer. Like Nightwing, he often fought crime alongside Batman. Green Arrow was the secret identity of the multimillionaire Oliver Queen.

Nightwing was surprised to see him. "Green Arrow? What are you doing here?"

"Nice to see you again too, kid," Green Arrow said with a grin. "The police subnet said there was an escape at Arkham, and I was in the neighborhood anyway."

"Really?" Nightwing asked skeptically.

"Not even close," admitted Green Arrow as he loaded an arrow into his bow. "But I didn't want to miss the fun."

He shot the arrow into the street below them. It sailed through the air and hit the trunk of the stolen convertible as the car passed by.

"Wait for it," said Green Arrow. "Three, two . . ."

BLAM!

The arrow made the trunk of the car explode and sent the convertible spinning out of control. Grundy frantically grasped the steering wheel as Silver Banshee turned to glare at the heroes. She took a deep breath, opened her mouth, and screamed.

"Jump!" yelled Nightwing as her sonic blast slammed into the building below them.

Both men somersaulted through the air and landed on a nearby rooftop, just as Silver Banshee screamed again, this time knocking the heroes off their feet.

"I think I got 'em that time," she said to Grundy.

"Bigger problem," said Grundy. "Object in mirror may be closer than it appears."

Silver Banshee turned around and saw the Batmobile, Batman's turbocharged crime-fighting vehicle, approaching fast. She inhaled deeply, trying to catch her breath.

Batman was driving, and Red Robin was in the passenger seat, pushing buttons on the computer in the vehicle's dashboard. Red Robin was a teen crime fighter, also known as Tim Drake. He was Batman's newest and youngest partner.

"Positive ID," said Red Robin. "It's Solomon Grundy and Silver Banshee."

"Let's see if they want a trick or a treat," said Batman as he accelerated and slammed the Batmobile against the back of the convertible. Silver Banshee was knocked to the floor of the car before she could scream again.

WHOMP!

Nightwing fired a grappling line that landed on top of the villains' car. He jumped over Grundy and collided with Silver Banshee in the backseat. He quickly reached for his two batons, and the tips of his weapons crackled with electricity. Silver Banshee grabbed Nightwing's wrists, so that he had to strain to move the batons toward her.

"Almost there!" called out Grundy from the front seat as they approached a tunnel.

"Step on it, will you?" grunted Silver Banshee as she slammed her knees into Nightwing's stomach and knocked him off balance.

Suddenly a bright green motorcycle zoomed onto the street and pulled up alongside the convertible. It was Green Arrow.

"Trick or treat, snowflake," he called out to Grundy.

Grundy ignored him and sped into the tunnel. As soon as the convertible and Green Arrow were inside, Silver Banshee opened her mouth and screamed.

Huge chunks of the tunnel's cement walls tumbled down and blocked the tunnel entrance completely. As the villains sped deeper into the tunnel, the Batmobile screeched to a halt outside, unable to enter the tunnel because of the rubble.

"Now what?" asked Red Robin.

"Time to do some drilling," said Batman as he pushed a button on the dashboard.

A panel opened at the front of the Batmobile, and a giant, spinning drill bit emerged and started carving through the debris.

Inside the tunnel the villains' car came to a stop as Green Arrow and Nightwing were hit by a sticky green glob that released a toxic gas. Green Arrow coughed and fell off his motorcycle, clasping his head in pain.

Nightwing couldn't move and watched helplessly as Silver Banshee delivered a punch, knocking him unconscious.

A man stepped out of the shadows at the side of the tunnel and stood over Green Arrow. It was the Scarecrow, the deadly villain who had once been a brilliant scientist named Dr. Jonathan Crane. During one of his experiments Crane had developed a fear-inducing gas that caused nightmares in the mind of anyone who inhaled it.

Green Arrow slowly opened his eyes. After one glance at the Scarecrow, he quickly closed them again and started screaming in fear, "No! Get away from me! Get away!"

"Boo!" the Scarecrow said. Then he walked over to

Grundy and Silver Banshee and glared at them. "What were you two *doing*?" he asked angrily.

"Don't be mad, Scarecrow," said Grundy with an embarrassed look.

"It was just a joyride," explained Silver Banshee.

"Was the plan too complicated for your pea-brains?" demanded the Scarecrow.

"Brain not made of peas," grumbled Grundy.

"You recall I told you to head directly to the meeting place after your escape? No antics? No tomfoolery? No shenanigans?"

"We remember," said Silver Banshee, sulking.

"*This*, my associates, is the very *definition* of shenanigans!" yelled the Scarecrow as he opened the car door and pushed Grundy aside. "Slide over. I'll drive."

The convertible zoomed out of the tunnel, leaving the two heroes sprawled on the ground.

It wasn't long before the Batmobile bored a hole through the rubble and Batman and Red Robin were able to drive into the tunnel and find their fallen friends.

"Arrow? Can you hear me?" asked Batman, gently tapping Green Arrow's face to wake him up.

Green Arrow moaned in pain and then focused on Batman's face.

"Oh, it's you," he said woozily. "Hey, Bats. I thought you might need some help."

Red Robin checked on Nightwing, who felt like he was waking up from a nightmare. Nightwing tossed what was left of the green goo over to Batman to analyze.

Batman ran a diagnostic scan on the green glob. "There are endoscopic traces of tetracycline and aerosol still in the air," he said. "That's residue from the Scarecrow's fear gas."

"Scarecrow, Silver Banshee, and Grundy are all working together?" asked Red Robin.

Batman looked grim. "Happy Halloween," he said.

CHAPTER 3

The moon was shining high above Gotham City on the night after Halloween. The bright billboards and video screens attached to the buildings cast a glow over the crowds in the streets. One giant monitor was broadcasting the evening news.

"Gotham City welcomes the cybernetic super hero Cyborg tonight," a newscaster said, smiling. "Cyborg is the guest of honor for Gotham Museum's unveiling of their new Inca exhibit. Cyborg's systems were instrumental in the location and excavation of this historic find!"

Cyborg was Victor Stone, a young man who had

become famous when several of his body parts had been replaced with computerized cyber limbs made of steel. The replacement body parts had been grafted to his skin to save his life after an accident, but they also gave him enhanced strength, vision, and endurance.

As the news broadcast continued, a police vehicle flew past the video screen.

"Dispatch, this is car four-oh-nine with our second sweep of sector twelve," a policeman said into his communication device. "No sign of the escaped inmates."

A voice from police headquarters replied, "Roger that, four-oh-nine. Keep looking."

The police craft floated past a tall building with a large video billboard featuring the *Angry Sasquatch* video game. The building was the headquarters for one of the most successful gaming companies in the nation, which had recently made headlines with the highly anticipated release of its first virtual-reality game, thought by many to be the best video game in the world.

Inside the building a young man was toiling away in the research laboratory. His name was Gogo Shoto, and although he was only nineteen years old, Gogo was a superstar programmer. Tonight he was wearing a metal virtual-reality helmet and frantically punching his arms in the air.

BAM!

Gogo was testing his virtual-reality game. In the game he had become a virtual Batman and was defeating four virtual villains with powerful punches. When the last villain standing pointed a gun at him, Batman quickly threw a Batarang at him, but it wobbled unsteadily as it flew through the air.

"No, no, no!" cried Gogo as he removed his virtual-reality helmet. "We need to smooth out the animation on the Batarang!"

Gogo pushed a series of buttons on a large console, and was surprised to hear a knock on the door. Looking up, he saw his coworker Ana.

"Okay, Gogo, I'm heading home," she said.

"No worries, Ana. I'm gonna debug the program for a little bit," he replied. "See you tomorrow."

Gogo slipped the helmet over his head again and started throwing punches in the air. One minute later Ana entered the room again.

"What did you forget?" Gogo asked as he removed the helmet.

Ana just smiled and walked stiffly over to Gogo.

"Ana, are you okay?" Gogo asked.

Suddenly Ana picked Gogo up by his shirt collar, punched him, and knocked him to the floor.

"Ana, what are you doing? Ow!" Gogo yelled as Ana hit him again.

Gogo ran from the lab and headed toward the cubicles in the next room. As he rounded a corner, he tripped, and landed with a crash on the floor. He saw with horror that he had just tripped over . . . Ana!

Gogo realized that whoever was chasing him, it wasn't the real Ana. He scrambled to his feet and ran down the hallway to the high-security server room where the main computers were located. As the fake Ana ran toward him, he punched a series of buttons on a control panel and a thick glass door slammed shut between them.

"That should hold her," Gogo said, and sighed with relief.

BLAM! BLAM!

The angry Ana clone was pounding on the glass door, which began to crack. Gogo ran to a nearby computer. His fingers flew across the keyboard as the crack in the glass door grew wider.

With one final keystroke Gogo altered the neon sign

atop the *Angry Sasquatch* building so that the sign displayed a giant Bat-Signal. Gogo knew that his only hope now was that Batman would see the sign and rescue him. But would the Dark Knight arrive in time?

CHAPTER 4

The Batcycle roared through the streets of Gotham City as Batman continued his search for Solomon Grundy, Silver Banshee, and the Scarecrow. The Dark Knight tapped a button on the vehicle's windshield, and instantly a video appeared of an elderly man with a thick mustache. It was Alfred Pennyworth, one of the few people who knew that Batman was Bruce Wayne, the wealthiest man in Gotham City. Alfred worked as Bruce Wayne's trusted butler and was also one of his most valued allies.

"Any news on the three villains since they disappeared last night?" asked Batman.

"Not a thing," replied Alfred. "No mention of them on the subnets, the dark web, or social media, sir."

"Keep at it. They didn't just disappear. Let me know the minute you find something."

"Of course, sir. And shall I press your tuxedo for the museum gala tomorrow?"

Batman looked up into the distance and saw the giant Bat-Signal shining atop the *Angry Sasquatch* building.

"I have to go," he said as the Batcycle zoomed toward the building. "I'm getting another call. Don't wait up."

Inside the building Gogo was in a state of panic as the fake Ana continued to slam her fists on the glass door.

"What is it you *want*?" Gogo yelled.

"You, Gogo Shoto," Ana replied coldly. "You are coming with me."

With one final blow the glass door shattered, and Ana stepped inside the room and grabbed Gogo.

"Let him go!" commanded a deep voice.

Gogo looked up with relief to see that Batman had also entered the room.

An evil smile crept over Ana's face. As she continued to hold on to Gogo, one of her fists began to morph into a giant hammer.

"I don't think so," she said as her arm suddenly stretched across the room and slammed into Batman's chest, knocking him across the room.

SMASH!

Ana began to laugh and ran down the hallway, carrying Gogo in her arms. As she ran, there was a loud slurping sound, and Ana began to transform. Now she was twice as large as before and was a slimy brown blob. It had been Clayface, the shape-shifting monster, all along!

Clayface held tightly on to Gogo as he smashed through a window forty stories above the ground, sprouted giant pterodactyl wings, and soared through the air. Batman had activated his glider cape and was not far behind.

Clayface landed with a splat in the middle of the street and turned to face Batman, who had just arrived next to him. Just then a giant truck roared into view, heading toward Clayface and Batman. With an evil grin Clayface launched a gooey geyser of clay at the truck, covering the vehicle's windshield. The driver swerved helplessly out of control, careening toward a young boy and his parents, who were watching the action, frozen in fear.

Thinking fast, Batman launched a Batarang into the

truck's wheel, giving it a flat tire and causing it to swerve away from the bystanders. With a screech the truck came to a halt.

"Thank you, Batman! Thank you!" cried the family as they ran over to the Dark Knight.

"Quick selfie?" asked the young boy as he held his cell phone next to Batman.

CLICK!

As the boy smiled into the camera, Batman's gaze was elsewhere. Clayface had gotten away.

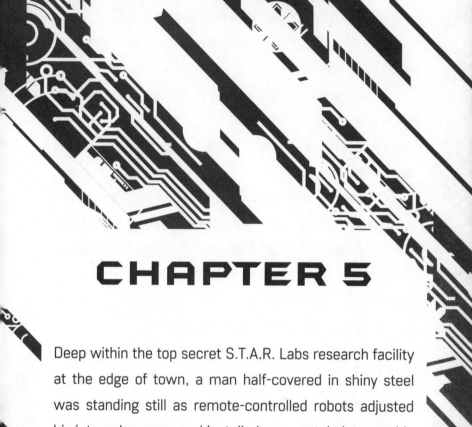

CHAPTER 5

Deep within the top secret S.T.A.R. Labs research facility at the edge of town, a man half-covered in shiny steel was standing still as remote-controlled robots adjusted his internal sensors and installed new metal plates on his body. When the robots had finished, Cyborg stretched his arms and grinned.

"Oooh, they tightened those sensors something fierce," he said. "Feels good, though."

Up in the observation deck at the far end of the room, Cyborg's father, Dr. Silas Stone, spoke to Cyborg over the loudspeaker.

"How are those upgrades interfacing, son?"

"Not bad, Pop. I'm incorporating them now. Let's see what we've got!"

Dr. Stone consulted a computer screen and said, "You now have three-hundred-and-sixty-degree tracking management. They'll interface nicely with your propulsion upgrades."

Cyborg was surprised. "Propulsion? I can *fly*?"

A panel clicked open at the back of Cyborg's mechanical suit to reveal two turbocharged jet wings. As the wings blasted into action, Cyborg started rocketing around the room.

"This is *amazing*!" he yelled happily.

"Let's try it with some targets," said Dr. Stone. He punched two buttons on his computer, and suddenly bright red laser circles surrounded Cyborg.

"Yeah, baby!" yelled Cyborg as he raised his arm to fire his wrist cannons at the moving circles, hitting each one.

Dr. Stone was chuckling at his son's exuberance when a grim-faced man wearing a trench coat entered the observation deck.

"Dr. Stone? I'm Police Commissioner Gordon," he said. "I just need a moment.

"Of course, Commissioner. I'll help however I can."

Gordon looked to where Cyborg was zooming through the air and said, "Sorry, Dr. Stone. It's not your help we need."

Cyborg looked up and saw his father with the commissioner.

"Pop? Is everything okay?"

"This is Police Commissioner Gordon. He needs your help," Dr. Stone replied.

"What can I do for you, Commissioner?

"I'm uploading some security footage to your sub-net now," Gordon said. He handed a small flash drive to Dr. Stone, who plugged it into his computer console so the video would appear both on-screen and in Cyborg's bionic eye.

"I've got it," Cyborg said. His bionic eye began to flicker as he viewed the download. All he could see was static.

"The footage was completely ruined," said Gordon. "We don't even know what they stole. According to the inventory everything is still there." He was hoping Cyborg might be able to recover the information.

Cyborg's eye flickered again as he got to work. "It looks like something overwhelmed the feed and blew it out. Let me grab the earlier footage and see if I can extrapolate some of the spatial telemetry."

Slowly the footage became more clear. The static on the screen cleared a bit, and Cyborg could see the walls of a research laboratory with a lot of security systems.

Cyborg told Gordon and Dr. Stone what he saw. "Infrared trip wires, laser cage, sonic alarms. . . . Someone wanted this place secured. Do you know which lab got hit?"

"Yes, it's an artificial intelligence research lab belonging to a Dr. Ivo," said Gordon.

Dr. Stone looked at the commissioner with surprise and said, "Ivo? I heard he recently made huge strides in the self-contained sequencing code."

"In English, if you don't mind, Doc," said Gordon.

"He created a fully functioning self-governing artificial intelligence," explained Stone.

"And that would be valuable?" asked Gordon.

Stone nodded and said, "An ultra-intelligent computer that could think and act for itself? I'd say so."

Cyborg had managed to clean up a few microseconds of the video, and two shadowy figures came into focus on-screen. "Let's take a look at our culprits," he said.

Gordon and Stone watched as Scarecrow and Silver

Banshee appeared on the screen in front of them.

"That fits," said Gordon. "The Scarecrow sprung her and Grundy out of Arkham last night."

Cyborg looked puzzled. "Why would a couple of fright freaks spend Halloween stealing an AI?" he wondered.

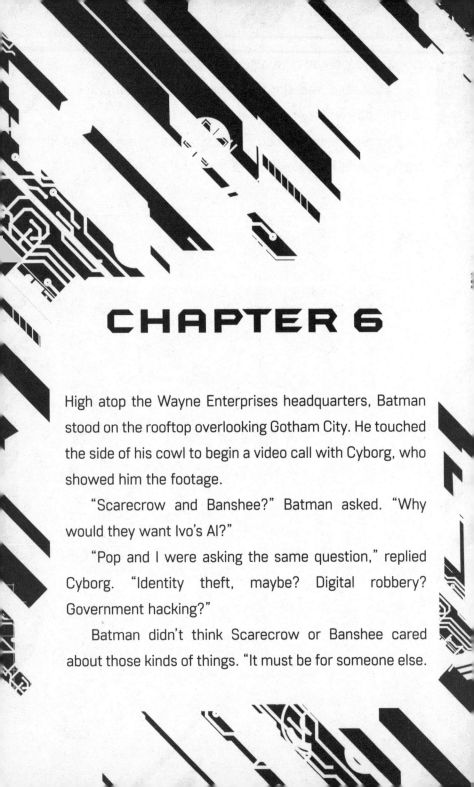

CHAPTER 6

High atop the Wayne Enterprises headquarters, Batman stood on the rooftop overlooking Gotham City. He touched the side of his cowl to begin a video call with Cyborg, who showed him the footage.

"Scarecrow and Banshee?" Batman asked. "Why would they want Ivo's AI?"

"Pop and I were asking the same question," replied Cyborg. "Identity theft, maybe? Digital robbery? Government hacking?"

Batman didn't think Scarecrow or Banshee cared about those kinds of things. "It must be for someone else.

Keep your eyes peeled, Cyborg," he said warily.

"Roger that, Batman. Cyborg out."

Meanwhile, outside Gotham City a man on a motorcycle traveled a desolate road that led to the city's power plant.

As he approached the gate, two bored guards inside the gatehouse were talking about what to order for dinner. Then they heard a knock.

"Pizza time," the man on the motorcycle said in a booming voice. "Piping hot pizza!"

"Did you already order a pizza?" asked one guard.

"Nah, did you?" asked the other.

The guards opened the door and took the pizza box. When they lifted the lid, there were only crumbs inside. The delivery man smiled. It was Solomon Grundy dressed in a pizza delivery outfit!

"Wait a second. Aren't you—" a guard began to say.

Grundy grabbed the two guards and knocked them together. They slumped to the ground.

"Grundy good actor!" the giant man said. He chuckled as he hopped back onto his motorcycle and headed for the main entrance to the atomic plant.

With a crash Grundy knocked the plant's door off its hinges and walked inside. The startled workers ran away, screaming.

"Pizza man! Who wants pizza?" bellowed Grundy.

Armed security guards ran toward Grundy. "Stay where you are!" commanded the leader of the guards.

Grundy smiled and started walking toward them.

"What's wrong? You no like pizza?" Grundy laughed as he knocked over four of the guards. Then he picked one guard up by his leg and started spinning him around like a rag doll. Grundy let go of the guard, sending him flying through the air and crashing into the remaining guards.

Grundy made his way down the hallway toward the center of the plant. When he came to a locked metal door, Grundy pulled back his massive arm and slammed his fist against it, knocking it open. Then he walked inside, toward the reactor.

Ignoring a sign that read ATOMIC BATTERY—DO NOT TOUCH! Grundy grabbed hold of a handle below the sign and began to pull the giant battery toward him. He hoisted the battery over his shoulder and walked back through the lobby of the plant.

As Grundy exited the building, he was unaware that he was being watched. Nightwing was perched on the rooftop and keeping a close eye on Grundy.

"Batman, I have a robbery in progress at the atomic power plant," Nightwing said into his communicator. "And guess who?"

The Dark Knight was zooming through the streets of Gotham City on the Batcycle, and replied, "I'm on my way."

An ice-cream truck was parked outside the power plant. With a grunt Grundy managed to lift the heavy battery and shove it inside the truck's back doors.

"What took you so long?" said an annoyed voice from the driver's seat. "I was starting to get antsy."

"They see through Grundy disguise," Grundy said sadly from outside the truck.

"Awww, have an ice cream. You'll feel better," said the voice, tossing an ice-cream cone to Grundy. Grundy smiled, then fell to the ground when one of Nightwing's electric batons knocked into him.

"Pretty re-*volt*-ing, eh, Grundy?" joked Nightwing as he landed on top of the ice-cream truck.

The driver of the ice-cream truck leaned out the window. It was the Joker, Gotham City's most dangerous villain. "Hey! *I'll* do the jokes around here, bird-boy. Now go perch somewhere else!" the Joker yelled to Nightwing.

"Uh-oh," Nightwing said when he saw the Joker.

"Take care of him, Grundy," yelled the Joker.

Grundy grabbed Nightwing as the Joker sped away in the truck. Nightwing reached down to the ground and grabbed one of his electrical batons. He twisted his body in the air and slammed the baton against Grundy, but within seconds the villain was on his feet again and swinging his giant fists at Nightwing. The hero jumped into the air to avoid the blows, but he was losing energy. One dangerous blow from Grundy could cripple him for life.

"Had enough?" Nightwing asked wearily.

"You funny," Grundy replied.

Grundy threw a punch that narrowly missed Nightwing, but before the hero could jump away, he was hit in the chest by Grundy's other hand. The impact sent Nightwing flying through the air and crashing into a wall. He slumped to the ground, unconscious, as Grundy smiled and hopped back onto his motorcycle.

"Me find Mr. Joker now," he said as he motored away.

CHAPTER 7

The Joker was laughing with glee as his ice-cream truck careened dangerously through the crowded streets of downtown Gotham City. He stopped laughing, though, when he looked in his rearview mirror and caught sight of someone in pursuit. Running just behind the truck was Ace, the Dark Knight's powerful robotic wolf.

"A robot wolf?" the Joker said with a sigh. "Oh, Bats, sometimes I think you're as crazy as I am!"

The Joker reached into his coat pocket, extracted six small digital explosive devices, and tossed them into the street. Ace deftly weaved as they exploded around him.

A large bat-shaped shadow fell over the Joker's truck, and the villain looked up to see Batman gliding through the air, his cape glider wings extended.

"All right!" the Joker said happily. "Let's get *down*!"

With that, he sharply turned the steering wheel and launched the truck off the side of an overpass. The vehicle sailed through the air and crashed onto a lower roadway, almost colliding with another car.

"Wheeeee!" screamed the Joker with joy.

Batman snapped his cape shut and landed on top of Ace, who had transformed from a robotic wolf into the Batcycle. Batman expertly piloted the vehicle over the edge of the overpass in pursuit of the Joker.

Within seconds Batman pulled up next to the Joker's truck.

"Stop this now, Joker!" commanded Batman.

The Joker smiled and said, as he held a hand to one ear, "I can't hear you. I'm going over the falls!"

Then he drove his truck through another overpass guardrail and crashed to the street below.

Batman followed him. "You can't outrun me, Joker!" he yelled.

"Outrun you? Where's the sport in that?" the Joker replied. He then extended his thin white hand out the window of the truck and pointed. "I'm waiting for him!"

Batman looked up to see Solomon Grundy on his motorcycle, heading straight toward the Batcycle.

SMASH!

Grundy's motorcycle slammed into the Batcycle and knocked Batman and his vehicle over the edge of the overpass and onto the street below. The Joker's truck skidded to a stop, and Grundy quickly climbed into it.

"Oh, Grundy, I could kiss you!" the Joker said happily. "In fact, I think I *will*! *MMMWAH!*" The Joker planted a big kiss on Grundy's cheek, and the giant monster blushed with embarrassment.

"Let's motor," said the Joker as the truck sped away. "Lots to do!"

Minutes later Batman shot a grapple from down below. It latched on to the guardrail, and he climbed back onto the overpass. The Joker had gotten away. But that wasn't the worst of it. Batman now realized that the Joker had teamed up with four of Gotham City's most dangerous villains. The Dark Knight was going to need a little help from his friends.

At the Gotham Harbor an iron gate blocked the entrance to the long-abandoned buildings of the Gotham Amusement

Park. In the park's heyday the citizens of Gotham City had flocked to the dazzling, brightly lit dock. Now the Ferris wheel and roller coaster were dark and deserted, and the buildings were covered with graffiti and crumbling into the harbor. Usually the only sounds to be heard were the lonely calls of seagulls.

Tonight, though, there was another sound: the cries of Gogo Shoto. He was tied up in the dark basement of one of the buildings, in the Joker's lair.

Grundy, Clayface, Scarecrow, and Silver Banshee all peered at Gogo.

"What's the angle?" demanded Clayface. "This fella's supposed to be *that* smart?"

"Apparently he's quite the hot hand in his field," said the Scarecrow.

Silver Banshee sneered and said, "He looks like a heapin' helping of hot *nothing* to me!"

Grundy licked his lips and said, "Now me hungry."

"Again? You just had pizza," said Silver Banshee.

"Grundy got fast metabolism," he replied.

Then Gogo spoke up. "Let me go, *please*! I'm just a video game designer!"

That was when they heard a cackling laugh. The other villains stepped aside as the Joker walked up to Gogo.

"I like your name, Gogo Shoto," the Joker said with a smile. "It's coo-coo-ca-ca-crazy."

"Y-y-you're the Joker," Gogo said nervously. "Please don't hurt me!"

"Hurt you? Don't talk twaddle, genius," the Joker replied. "I need you!"

The Joker smacked Gogo's cheek with his hand.

"You see," the Joker continued as he leered at Gogo, "I'm going to play this *amazing* practical joke on Gotham City. And I need *your* help to do it!"

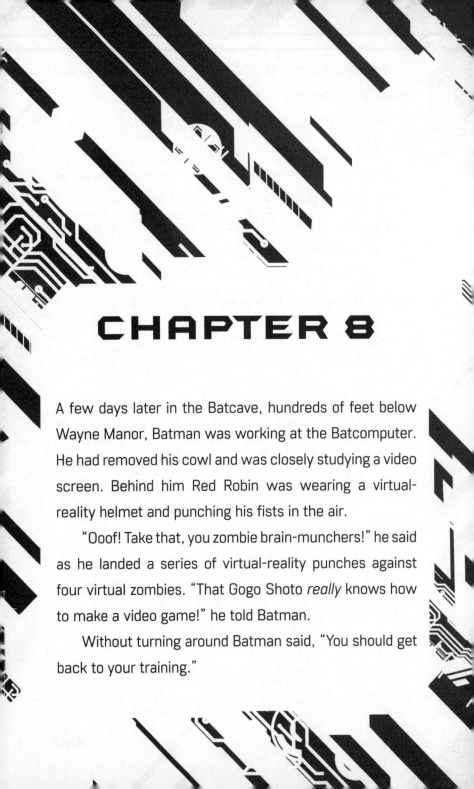

CHAPTER 8

A few days later in the Batcave, hundreds of feet below Wayne Manor, Batman was working at the Batcomputer. He had removed his cowl and was closely studying a video screen. Behind him Red Robin was wearing a virtual-reality helmet and punching his fists in the air.

"Ooof! Take that, you zombie brain-munchers!" he said as he landed a series of virtual-reality punches against four virtual zombies. "That Gogo Shoto *really* knows how to make a video game!" he told Batman.

Without turning around Batman said, "You should get back to your training."

Red Robin could barely hear Batman over the sound of his virtual battle, and he replied, "Yeah, I know! This is *great* training. Watch me clear this level!"

Batman frowned and punched a button on the computer. Images and files on four villains appeared on his monitor. "Grundy, Scarecrow, Clayface, and Silver Banshee," he said.

Red Robin removed his helmet and peered over Batman's shoulder. "That's a frightful foursome if I've ever seen one."

Batman stared at the data and said, "Each of them is a powerful enemy. Why join forces?"

"And why follow the Joker?" added Red Robin.

Batman punched a button, and the image of Gogo Shoto filled the screen. "It's all tied to Gogo Shoto. Why kidnap a video game designer?" he pondered.

"Gogo's more than just a designer," said Red Robin. "He's an artist. His open-world games let you push the boundaries of human experience. You can do anything. There's a rumor that in his next game you'll be able to be . . ." Red Robin paused, embarrassed.

"Be who?" demanded Batman.

Red Robin shrugged and said with a grin, "Batman."

"Multiple Batmans? What a terrifying thought," said

a voice from the other end of the Batcave. It was Alfred, approaching with a tray of tea. "Just imagine hand-washing all of those capes," he said with a shudder as he placed the tray next to the Batcomputer. "The tea is Darjeeling. The sandwiches are turkey. The pills are for your headache," he said.

"Thanks, Alfred," said Batman. "I don't know what I'd do without you."

"For starters you'd wash your own cape," Alfred replied. "I've laid out your tuxedo and shined your shoes for the gala opening of the new Inca exhibit at the museum tonight."

Batman frowned. "That's tonight already?"

"Yes, sir," said Alfred. "And since the dig was under-written by the Wayne Foundation, it would be *most* impo-lite for Bruce Wayne not to make an appearance." As usual, Alfred wanted to make sure Batman did the right thing.

Batman sighed and said, "All right. Tell Dick and Oliver I want them there too. I've got a bad feeling about this party."

"Master Tim as well?" asked Alfred.

Red Robin was lowering the helmet over his head again and said, "Oh no! I hate the museum. Why would

I want to look at a bunch of boring old-fashioned ways to do things when I have all of this cool tech to do it *for* me?"

"The gala is in an hour," Alfred said to Batman. "Try not to be late."

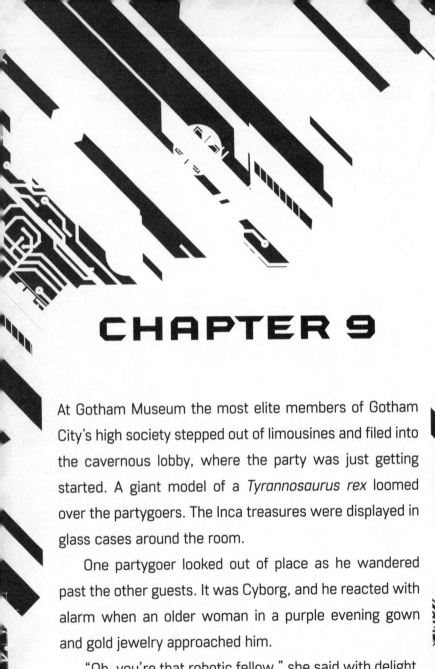

CHAPTER 9

At Gotham Museum the most elite members of Gotham City's high society stepped out of limousines and filed into the cavernous lobby, where the party was just getting started. A giant model of a *Tyrannosaurus rex* loomed over the partygoers. The Inca treasures were displayed in glass cases around the room.

One partygoer looked out of place as he wandered past the other guests. It was Cyborg, and he reacted with alarm when an older woman in a purple evening gown and gold jewelry approached him.

"Oh, you're that robotic fellow," she said with delight.

"Robotman?" she added with some uncertainty.

"Cyborg," he replied politely.

"No, that's not it," she said as she shook her head.

"Why don't you just call me Victor?"

"Well, if you insist," she said, and wrapped her arm around his.

"Now, Gladys, are you bothering our guest of honor?" Bruce teased the woman. Then he introduced himself to Cyborg. "Cyborg, I'm Bruce Wayne. I haven't had the pleasure in person yet."

"It's a real honor, Mr. Wayne," said Cyborg as he shook Bruce's hand.

"I suppose we have you to thank for these amazing Inca findings," Gladys said to Bruce.

"Oh no," he replied. "I just signed the check. It's Cyborg that's the big hero. His radar told us where to dig."

Gladys turned to Cyborg and asked, "Am I to understand that you discovered some kind of magical Inca energy gem?"

"It's rhodochrosite, also called the Inca Rose Stone," said Cyborg. "It's not magic as much as it's supposed to be an excellent conductor of energy."

Just then Bruce Wayne spotted Oliver Queen and

Dick Grayson across the room, and excused himself so that he could join them.

"Gentlemen, finally I found you. How are things, Oliver?" he said heartily.

"You know me. Living the life, living the dream . . . ," he said loudly. "Dick and I were talking about what we did for Halloween," Oliver went on. Then, after making sure that no one was eavesdropping, Oliver lowered his voice and said, "Any word on our boo crew?"

"Not a thing," said Bruce. "How's security here?"

"Commissioner Gordon has had it locked up tight since this afternoon," replied Dick.

"You expecting Mr. Funny Business tonight?" asked Oliver.

"After stealing a computer expert, an AI, and a battery, it fits the pattern," said Bruce. "Stay alert. The Clown is up to something."

Soon all of the guests had arrived, and a spotlight shone on a man standing at a podium in front of the *T. rex*.

"Good evening, Ladies and Gentlemen. I'm Houston Raines, the Channel Six weatherman and tonight's master of ceremonies," he said to polite applause from the crowd. "There are a lot of people who made this amazing Inca discovery happen. Bruce Wayne for one. Big hand for

Mr. Wayne! Also Cyborg, who actually found the amazing and historic Inca energy gem. But I also want to extend a big thank-you to—"

Before he could finish his sentence, the Joker suddenly appeared at his side and shoved Raines to the ground.

"*Me!*" the Joker said with a laugh. "Howdy, Gotham City. Did you *miss* me?"

As the crowd gasped and a few partygoers started running from the room, members of the Gotham City SWAT Team pointed their laser guns at the Joker.

"Gentlemen, you cut me to the quick," the Joker called out. "I don't want any trouble!" The Joker then pointed to the giant *Tyrannosaurus rex* model standing above him, and with an evil smile he said, "Now—my friend, he *loves* trouble!"

ROAAAAAR! The dinosaur suddenly came to life and with a menacing roar displayed his razor-sharp teeth.

In a panic, guests stumbled over one another, desperately trying to escape.

A dozen laser blasts sailed right through the dinosaur. It continued to move toward the frightened partygoers.

Cyborg was fighting his way through the crowd, and then he remembered his new power of flight. He quickly extended his turbocharged wings and soared into the air.

"You're going extinct, lizard-breath," he called out to the dinosaur, and fired his white-noise cannon at the creature.

BLAM!

The cannon blast soared harmlessly right through the dinosaur.

Then the *T. rex* swung its head and rammed it into Cyborg, hurling him across the room.

BOOM!

An explosive arrow fired by Green Arrow hit the dinosaur in its nose, causing the giant creature to stumble backward. It quickly recovered and let out an even louder roar. Bruce, Dick, and Oliver had all changed into their suits, and now Batman, Nightwing, and Green Arrow ran toward the dinosaur.

They didn't notice the Joker smashing the glass display case around the Inca Rose Stone and grabbing the gem.

"Oooh, what a belt buckle you'd make," the Joker said as he held the stone. "It's a shame I have other plans for you." When he looked up, he saw Batman and ran off, with Batman close behind him.

The *T. rex* knocked into Green Arrow and Nightwing.

While they were recovering, the dinosaur transformed into a mass of what looked like brown putty.

It was Clayface, and once his transformation was complete, he quickly took the form of Gladys, the woman who had talked with Cyborg earlier that night, and blended into the crowd.

"Where did Clayface go?" yelled Commissioner Gordon. "Anyone got eyes on him?"

Clayface had already exited the museum and joined Solomon Grundy, Silver Banshee, and the Scarecrow in the stolen red convertible. Seconds later the Joker came running down the museum steps carrying the Inca Rose Stone.

"I don't think we got room for you in the car, boss," said Grundy nervously.

"Never mind. I brought my own," the Joker said as he pressed a button on a small device. A remote-controlled Joker-cycle roared into view.

"Let's ride!" he called out with a wild laugh.

Batman emerged from the museum just in time to see the five villains speed away.

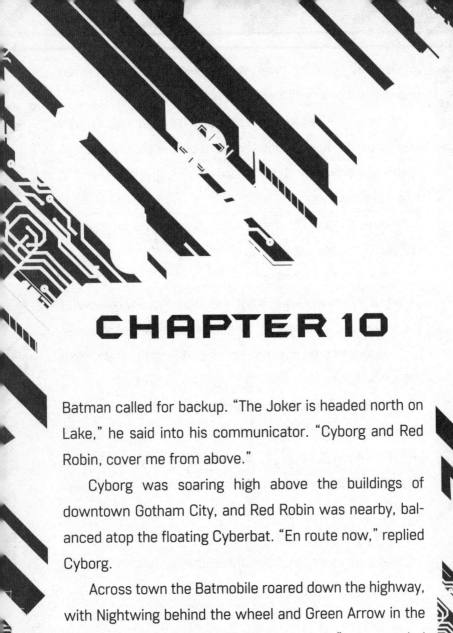

CHAPTER 10

Batman called for backup. "The Joker is headed north on Lake," he said into his communicator. "Cyborg and Red Robin, cover me from above."

Cyborg was soaring high above the buildings of downtown Gotham City, and Red Robin was nearby, balanced atop the floating Cyberbat. "En route now," replied Cyborg.

Across town the Batmobile roared down the highway, with Nightwing behind the wheel and Green Arrow in the passenger seat. "Nightwing, Green Arrow," commanded Batman over the comm, "cut them off!"

"You got it, Bats," replied Green Arrow as Nightwing stepped on the gas pedal.

The Joker was driving his motorcycle through the streets of downtown Gotham City, weaving in and out of traffic.

"This is King Clown," he said into his own communicator device. "Anyone got their ears on?"

The Scarecrow responded, "Dr. Crane here. We read you, Joker."

The Joker looked up in the air and smiled as he saw Red Robin tailing him close behind.

"Doc, I've developed a tail I want to get rid of," said the Joker as he took a sharp left turn and zoomed into an alley. Red Robin tilted the Cyberbat to follow the Joker, just as the convertible full of villains appeared on the street.

"Uh-oh," said Red Robin as he noticed the new arrivals.

Silver Banshee opened her mouth and let out a piercing scream. Red Robin dipped the Cyberbat to avoid the impact of her sonic boom, which bounced off a building.

CRASH!

The Batmobile zoomed into view and smashed into the side of the villains' convertible, knocking the car off course for a few moments.

"It's *so* hard to find good help these days," said the Joker with a sigh as he pushed a button on the dashboard of his Joker-cycle. A small panel opened at the rear of his vehicle, revealing three missile launchers.

BLAM! BLAM! BLAM!

Nightwing turned the wheel of the Batmobile sharply to avoid the three exploding rockets.

"Two can play at that game!" said Clayface as he stretched his giant arms behind him and started firing gooey brown geysers of clay at both the Batmobile and Red Robin. One glob of clay smacked into Red Robin and knocked him off the Cyberbat, but he quickly got back on and flew into the air.

The Joker looked up just in time to see Cyborg flying directly toward him. The villain quickly swerved his cycle to avoid the impact.

"Close, but no cigar, Tin Man!" said the Joker with a laugh.

"I've got him!" Clayface declared as he stood up in the convertible and extended two large brown wings from his back. Within seconds the monster was flying through the air and slammed into Cyborg. Before Cyborg could escape, Clayface encased the hero within his gooey arms.

Batman raced over on the Batcycle, but the Joker spun his bike around and started shooting laser blasts.

ZAP! ZAP!

Batman quickly sped away to avoid the blasts.

As the Joker continued to speed through the streets, he reached into his coat pocket and extracted a communicator device. A grinning Joker avatar appeared on the device's video screen. When the Joker tapped its face, the avatar spoke.

"Yes, Mr. Joker?" it asked in a squeaky voice.

"Do it," commanded the Joker.

Suddenly the streetlights, traffic signals, neon signs, and lights all over downtown turned off. All the office buildings and shop windows went dark.

The Batcycle began to shudder violently, causing Batman to lose his balance and tumble from the vehicle. He barely managed to avoid a collision with the Batmobile, which was careening wildly down the street as Nightwing frantically swung the car's unresponsive steering wheel.

SMASH!

Batman watched in dismay as the Batmobile crashed into the side of a building. He ran over to the damaged vehicle. Luckily, Nightwing and Green Arrow weren't hurt.

"What happened?" Batman asked.

"No clue," said Nightwing. "Everything just started shaking."

"I knew I should have driven!" muttered Green Arrow.

Nightwing ignored this comment and said, "It's like all the machines went haywire!"

A worried look came over Batman's face, and he said, "Red Robin!"

The three heroes looked up to see that Red Robin was flying through the air on his Cyberbat, but it was no longer working. As it wobbled and lost power, the young hero began to fall.

Batman reached for his grappling gun to help Red Robin, but Green Arrow stepped in instead.

"I've got him," declared Green Arrow as he shot two arrows into the sky. Both arrows pierced Red Robin's cape and then sent the young hero flying into a nearby wall.

"Ooof!" said Red Robin as he slid down to the ground.

"You good, kid?" asked Green Arrow.

Red Robin held his head in pain and said, "Yeah. Gonna need to walk that one off."

Batman walked over to the Batcycle, which had transformed back into Ace, the cyber wolf. The robotic creature was struggling on the ground, its lights flickering, and it was cackling with a strange, mechanical laugh.

Green Arrow peered at Ace, and then at Batman. "Hold on. Is your motorcycle *laughing*?" he asked.

"It must be a computer virus," Batman said grimly.

Nightwing looked up into the air and said, "Computer virus? Oh no. Where's Cyborg?"

At that moment Cyborg was battling the winged Clayface high above Gotham City. Cyborg slammed his fist into Clayface's stomach.

SQUISH!

Just as Cyborg was about to reach back and deliver another powerful blow, he paused. A smile came over Cyborg's face, and he started chuckling. Soon he was doubled over in laughter. He was laughing so hard that his internal circuits started to overheat. Cyborg swayed in the air, tilting wildly out of control. He was guffawing loudly as he fell to the ground and landed with a crash on top of a parked car. He then rolled onto the street, still giggling and helplessly waving his robotic arms in the air.

Seconds later Clayface gathered Cyborg into his gooey arms and hopped into the red convertible, where the three other villains were waiting. The car soon sped away through the darkened streets of Gotham City.

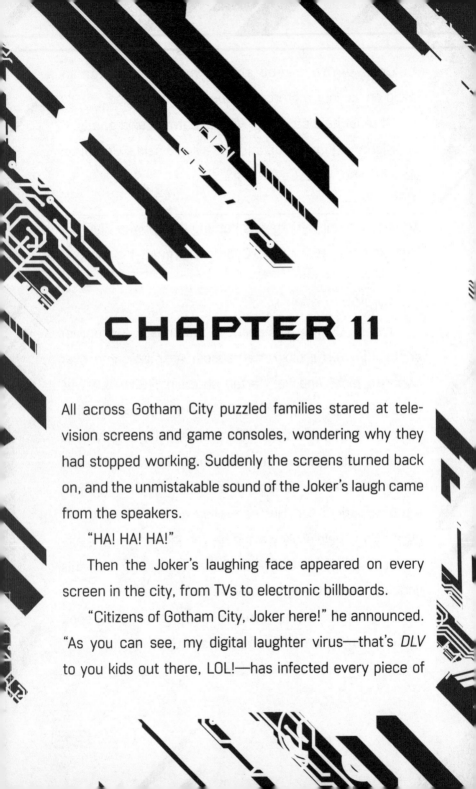

CHAPTER 11

All across Gotham City puzzled families stared at television screens and game consoles, wondering why they had stopped working. Suddenly the screens turned back on, and the unmistakable sound of the Joker's laugh came from the speakers.

"HA! HA! HA!"

Then the Joker's laughing face appeared on every screen in the city, from TVs to electronic billboards.

"Citizens of Gotham City, Joker here!" he announced. "As you can see, my digital laughter virus—that's *DLV* to you kids out there, LOL!—has infected every piece of technology in the entire city. Power plants, traffic lights, everything on the digital grid now belongs to me. Nothing around here works unless I say it works," he continued. "Which makes me king of Gotham City!"

The Joker then placed a jewel-encrusted gold crown on his head, wrapped a thick fur cape around his shoulders, and grasped an ornate scepter. He tapped the scepter in his palm as he leaned closer to the camera.

"And believe me, there are gonna be some *changes* around here. For starters, Solomon Grundy"—the camera pulled back to reveal Grundy, dressed in an ill-fitting police officer's cap and suit—"is now the sheriff of Gotham City," the Joker said, "which means, kids, he runs the police force!"

Grundy squinted into his open palm, clearly reading something that he had written on his hand.

"I . . . happily . . . accept . . . this . . . poison," he read slowly.

The Joker shouted, "*Position!* You accept the *position*!"

Grundy shrugged and agreed, "Right! Poison!"

The Joker shook his head with disgust and said, "Let me introduce the rest of my cabinet. Presenting the new Baron of Candy and Ice Cream—mostly because he looks like melted chocolate—Clayface!"

Clayface stared into the camera and then morphed into George Washington.

"I cannot tell a lie. I am proud to serve!" he said.

The camera turned to Silver Banshee, but the Joker changed his mind and moved on to his next announcement.

"Hey!" protested Silver Banshee.

The Joker ignored her. "Finally, here is our guy who handles everything else—the Scarecrow," he said.

The Scarecrow was wearing black glasses over his mask and was standing in front of a financial chart. "Gothamites, since all banks, ATMs, and accounts are offline, there is no money anymore," the Scarecrow said. "So, I will be *redesigning* the economic system. Information will be our new currency! Spot a hero? Tell us, and I'll let you use your car for an hour. Neighbors planning a revolution? Tell us, and I'll let you watch TV for three nights."

The camera whipped back to the Joker, and he leaned in close to say, "Those are just a few of the new ground rules. Don't worry. There are *many* more to come. King Joker over and *out*!"

Every screen and every light in Gotham City switched off, and the streets and homes were plunged into total darkness.

CHAPTER 12

Only one light was shining in the city. It was a yellow oval piercing the dark clouds above Gotham City's buildings. In the middle of the yellow light was the emblem of a bat. Commissioner Gordon and two police officers had lit a fire below the Bat-Signal, the large machine on the roof of Gotham City police headquarters that projected the silhouetted shape of a bat into the sky to call for help from Batman. The light from the flickering flames was just enough to shine the bat emblem dimly in the night-time sky.

"You think it's enough?" one police officer asked the

others with skepticism. "Maybe he can't see it."

"Or maybe he's just not coming," said the other.

Gordon scanned the skies and said, "He's coming."

Just then Batman stepped out of the shadows and said, "I'm here."

"Batman, thank goodness. All of our tech is down—cars, communicators, even our weapons that have micro-chips coded to our fingerprints. We're back to the Dark Ages here."

"I know," Batman replied. "It's a computer virus. We're trying to hack it now."

Gordon shook his head and added, "That's not the worst of it. With Grundy as the sheriff . . ."

His voice trailed off, and Batman said, "He busted you back down to a street cop, right?"

Gordon nodded and said, "Yeah. His idea of a joke, I'm sure. I'm lucky the old uniform fits."

"Do what you can from the inside. Keep the peace at all costs," Batman said as he walked to the edge of the rooftop and aimed his grappling gun. "I'll be in touch."

Seconds later Batman had sailed over the edge of the building and disappeared into the darkness.

Back in the Batcave, Alfred brought in small generators that cast a warm glow in the gloomy cavern and could provide some power.

"I'm certain you don't need me to mention this, but these gas generators are only a temporary solution . . . at best," he said.

"We've got limited battery power as well," said Nightwing, plugging a light into one of the generators.

"It would have been nice to have some solar power," said Green Arrow, thinking of solar panels. "If Gotham City ever got any sun, that is."

"It doesn't matter. Nothing digital works," said Red Robin.

"Plus, the Clown has put a bounty on our heads," added Green Arrow. "If you snap a pic of one of us now, you get an hour of video games."

Red Robin looked forlornly at his dark game system in the corner. "An hour, huh?" he said hopefully. "Really? A whole hour?"

"Don't even *joke*!" Green Arrow warned the youngster.

"Joker's got Cyborg, controls technology," Nightwing said to Batman, "and now he's turning Gotham City against us. How do we fight that?"

"We find him," Batman said grimly.

Green Arrow shook his head and said flatly, "Great. Why didn't I think of that, Bats. But *how*?"

THUMP!

Batman dropped a heavy pile of maps, books, and photos on the table.

"We get smart," he said, "and do it the old-fashioned way."

Green Arrow sighed as he reached for a map and said, "Where do we start?"

"In his original form, Clayface attracts debris," said Batman. He explained that if they examined the dirt, dust, and debris stuck in the goo that Clayface had left behind, they might be able to find a clue about where Clayface and the others were hiding.

"There's still plenty on Red Robin," said Green Arrow as he removed a bit of Clayface's goo from Red Robin's tunic.

"Nightwing, I've been collecting audio of Joker's dispatches," Batman said as he handed over a small recording device. "See if there's a clue to where he's broadcasting from."

Batman continued, "Red Robin, I want to know why he needed the Inca Rose gem."

"Aye, aye, captain," responded the young hero. "What are you gonna do?"

Suddenly the Batcomputer screen lit up and was filled with an image of the Joker, still wearing his cape and crown.

"Greetings, my loyal subjects. King Joker the First here with a special offer for all of you boys and girls," he cried out with a laugh. "I know how much you all love me, so I'm going to let you throw me a parade! And the theme of the parade is going to be . . . *me*! I want to see Joker balloons, Joker costumes, Joker floats. We're going to show the entire world how great Joker-Town is!"

The screen suddenly went dark. Batman turned to the other heroes.

"I want results in two hours," he said.

Exactly two hours later the heroes assembled in front of a giant map that Batman was studying.

The Dark Knight didn't even look up as he said, "Arrow?"

"Let me say that Clayface sucks up more particles than a vacuum cleaner," Green Arrow said as he shook his head with disgust. "Other than your everyday dirt and grime, here's the headline. I found a higher-than-average concentration of mineral salts, mollusk shells, and coral-line algae."

"Mineral salts are sea spray. Seashells and algae are biologic components that make up sand," Batman said as he took a pen and circled an area on the map at the edge of Gotham City. "Good job, Arrow. That puts them somewhere on the coastline. Red Robin?"

"The Inca Rose gem is an energy conductor," replied Robin. "The Joker is probably using it to boost the transmission signal for his broadcasts, but the source would still have to be centralized."

Batman then circled an area of the coast that was close to Gotham City.

"Better," he said. "Nightwing?"

Nightwing was holding a cell phone in his hand.

"What is *that* thing?" asked Red Robin.

"It's called a cell phone," explained Nightwing. "People used them to listen to music and talk to friends and family."

"Oh, *old*-school," replied Red Robin.

"On every Joker dispatch there's a slight reoccurring noise." Nightwing had isolated the sound from the rest of the noise and turned up the volume. He touched the cell phone's screen, and the soft clanging sound of a bell began to play.

"What is that? A church bell?" asked Green Arrow.

"It's a navigational buoy. They surround the docks," said Batman as he drew a new, smaller circle on the map and then brought out a photo. "Okay, this is the Joker's cycle. I knew the gorilla on the cycle looked familiar, but at first I couldn't place it. It's made of parts from a carnival ride that was condemned a long time ago. That ride used to be here." Batman drew one final, small circle. "The abandoned fairgrounds on the Old Gotham Pier," he said. "Let's go."

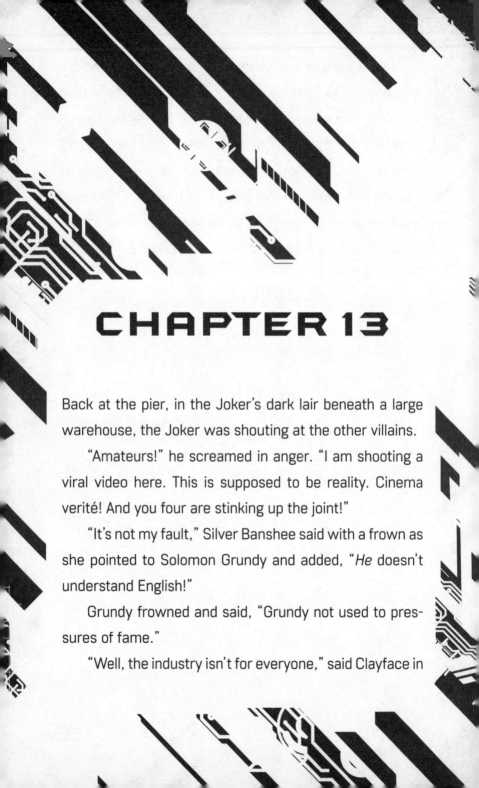

CHAPTER 13

Back at the pier, in the Joker's dark lair beneath a large warehouse, the Joker was shouting at the other villains.

"Amateurs!" he screamed in anger. "I am shooting a viral video here. This is supposed to be reality. Cinema verité! And you four are stinking up the joint!"

"It's not my fault," Silver Banshee said with a frown as she pointed to Solomon Grundy and added, "*He* doesn't understand English!"

Grundy frowned and said, "Grundy not used to pressures of fame."

"Well, the industry isn't for everyone," said Clayface in

his gravelly voice as he motioned toward the Scarecrow.

"*Me?* Please!" said the Scarecrow indignantly. "You're chewing scenery so fast, I'm amazed we have any left standing."

"That's *enough*!" shouted the Joker as he stormed past them and headed toward the exit. "Save it for the video. You four keep practicing. I'll be back."

The Joker walked outside the warehouse and hopped onto his Joker-cycle. As the villain zoomed away, Batman stepped out of the shadows and raised one hand in the air. Green Arrow was watching from high atop the carnival's Ferris wheel, and on Batman's signal he drew back an arrow in his bow and fired it. The arrow crashed through the window of the warehouse and landed inches away from the four villains.

"It's the archer!" said the Scarecrow alarmed. "They've found us."

KER-BLAM!

Suddenly the arrow exploded, flooding the room with a thick knockout gas. The coughing villains stumbled their way out of the warehouse, just as another arrow zipped through the air and bounced harmlessly off Grundy's shoulder.

"There!" Grundy said, pointing his pals toward Green

Arrow, who was standing on top of the Ferris wheel.

"I'll take care of him," Banshee said, and she let loose a piercing scream.

"Uh-oh," said Green Arrow. A Ferris wheel car below him exploded from the impact of her voice.

"Whoa, that's some temper," he said as he jumped to a lower car.

Silver Banshee smiled grimly as she started moving closer, preparing to emit a scream that would bring Green Arrow crashing to the ground.

"Those other heroes are skulking around here somewhere, I can tell," the Scarecrow said. "Search every inch of this place. Find them. Eliminate them!"

As the villains separated to search the fairgrounds, Red Robin crawled along the warehouse roof. He slid open a skylight and dropped with a thud to the floor of the building. The sound caught the attention of Clayface, who smiled and made his way back into the warehouse. As he walked through the dark room, he quickly transformed into an uncanny replica of Batman.

"Hello? Anyone in here?" he called out.

Red Robin was out of Clayface's view, behind some wooden crates, but he was surprised to hear the Dark Knight's voice.

"Come out, come out, wherever you are!" said Clayface.

Red Robin realized that Clayface was impersonating Batman, and reached into his Utility Belt to extract a Batarang. He tossed the Batarang over to the far side of the warehouse.

CLUNK!

Then Red Robin watched as the fake Batman ran toward the noise.

"Ah. You're over there, my fellow hero," Clayface called out.

Red Robin moved quickly down a hallway, and then paused. He heard the muffled sounds of someone crying for help, and discovered Gogo Shoto tightly bound in ropes. Red Robin removed the gag from Gogo's mouth.

"Get me outta here!" Gogo pleaded.

"You ain't taking him anywhere," Clayface announced, surprising Gogo and Red Robin. He had run back across the warehouse and was now in his usual, gooey form. He pounded his fists.

"We'll see about that!" replied the hero as he prepared to defend himself against Clayface's giant arms.

Clayface threw a punch, and Red Robin did a quick backflip. The young hero then flung two small Batarangs at his opponent, but they sank with a harmless squish into his body.

Clayface turned one arm into a giant sword and started swinging it. Red Robin jumped to the left and right, deftly staying out of reach of the blade. He then jumped into the air, did a perfect somersault, and landed on Clayface's shoulder. Red Robin watched as his boot sank into Clayface's body.

The villain smiled and said, "That's some bad luck there, bird-boy!"

He then yanked Red Robin into the air and threw him across the room. Red Robin crashed headfirst into a pile of bumper cars.

As Red Robin rubbed his forehead and sat up, he saw with dismay that there were now *two* Gogo Shotos standing next to each other. Clayface had morphed himself into a perfect replica of Gogo.

"Quick, you have to get me out of here!" said one Gogo.

"No, he's lying. It's *me* you have to get out of here!" said the other.

"Stop it! You are not me!" said one Gogo.

"*You* stop it. I'm the real Gogo!" said the other.

"Well?" asked one Gogo as he turned to Red Robin.

"Can't you do something?" he asked exasperatedly.

"Look, one of you is Gogo and one of you is Clayface," said Red Robin.

"He's Clayface!" both Gogos said, and pointed at each other.

Suddenly Red Robin smiled. As he moved closer to the two young men, he surreptitiously removed two gas bombs from his Utility Belt.

"By the way," Red Robin said, "how do you kill the flamethrower zombie boss in *Armageddon Days 4*?"

One Gogo quickly replied with the correct answer.

The other Gogo looked puzzled for a moment and then quickly added, "Right. . . . I knew that! I was just . . ."

Red Robin took a step closer as that Gogo morphed back into Clayface and said with a roar, "I'm going to pound you into mush!"

Red Robin deftly tossed the two gas bombs into Clayface's open mouth. With a startled look the villain let out a loud burp. "I don't feel so good," he said, and fell to the ground.

Red Robin and Gogo both exhaled sighs of relief, and then Red Robin turned to Gogo.

"So how do you get across the minefield in level nine, then?" Red Robin asked.

"Are you *seriously* asking me that now?" Gogo said with disbelief. "Um, well, you trade your munitions for the map in the canteen."

"Oh, of course!" said Red Robin. "Why didn't I think of that?"

CHAPTER 14

Solomon Grundy was stomping through the deserted fair-grounds and saw Batman run into a ride called the Tunnel of Love, which was covered in pink hearts.

Grundy followed him, and when he reached the ride, he pushed a button on a power box. Suddenly the Tunnel of Love was working again, lit up by hundreds of red lightbulbs. Grundy eased his giant body into one of the wooden boats that was bobbing in the tunnel's waterway. He followed Batman into the ride as the sounds of soft, romantic music played in the background.

Grundy spotted Batman ahead, standing in a boat at

the front of the line. The giant villain hopped from one boat to another toward the Dark Knight.

BLAM!

Batman fired a grapple that wrapped around Grundy's arm. Batman pulled the cord and made Grundy hit himself in the face. Then Batman pulled it again, and Grundy fell into the water.

After a moment of silence Grundy punched his arm through the floor of the boat Batman was standing in. As the two fought, the boat broke into splinters. Batman hopped to the platform on the side of the water, while Grundy stood in the water, which came up to only his waist. Batman grabbed a Batarang.

"That won't stop me, Batman!" Grundy yelled.

The Dark Knight reached back and threw the Batarang, not at Grundy but at the heavy wire that was attached to the nearby wall. The Batarang sliced the wire in half, and the wire shot off electric sparks.

"Lights out, Grundy," said Batman as the electric wire fell into the water.

Within seconds Grundy fell backward and groaned.

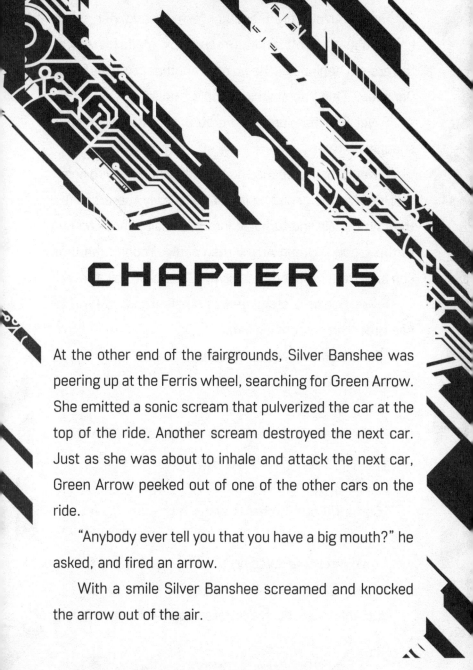

CHAPTER 15

At the other end of the fairgrounds, Silver Banshee was peering up at the Ferris wheel, searching for Green Arrow. She emitted a sonic scream that pulverized the car at the top of the ride. Another scream destroyed the next car. Just as she was about to inhale and attack the next car, Green Arrow peeked out of one of the other cars on the ride.

"Anybody ever tell you that you have a big mouth?" he asked, and fired an arrow.

With a smile Silver Banshee screamed and knocked the arrow out of the air.

Green Arrow fired another arrow, and her voice knocked that one off target. Green Arrow made his way to the ground behind her. He pointed another arrow at Silver Banshee. "Don't do anything stupid," he said.

Silver Banshee lunged to grab Green Arrow's bow. It snapped in two.

Silver Banshee opened her mouth wide, ready to finish off Green Arrow once and for all. He quickly somersaulted through the air and tumbled into the villain, knocking her to the ground. Green Arrow then sadly dropped the broken bow from his hands and said, "Good night, old friend."

Silver Banshee staggered to her feet just in time to see Green Arrow running away.

"Go ahead and leg it, coward. I'll catch up with you soon enough!" she yelled.

Green Arrow was standing in the shadows near the abandoned galleries of the midway games. Silver Banshee was walking down a nearby corridor.

"Come on out, archer. I won't hurt you . . . *much!*" she called out.

Green Arrow pondered his options and muttered to himself, "Think, Oliver, think. You can't *throw* arrows at her."

Just then he noticed a tattered booth for the carnival's

baseball tossing game. A dozen musty baseballs were still piled on the counter. He ran over to the counter and grabbed the baseballs.

"Found you!" said Silver Banshee. "You can't hide from me."

Green Arrow moved confidently to the center of the midway. His quiver was filled with baseballs, and he tossed one into the air and caught it.

"Good thing I'm not," he said.

"This is almost too easy," Silver Banshee said with an evil smile. She opened her mouth to inhale.

BLAM!

She was hit with a baseball, and scowled.

BLAM!

Another ball bounced off a nearby wall and crashed into her again.

Silver Banshee quickly recovered, and just as another ball was about to make contact, she emitted a scream and knocked the ball off course.

Green Arrow's hands were now a blur, extracting baseballs from his quiver and lobbing them at the villain.

"Here's what I realized, Banshee," he said as he pulled back his arm for one last big pitch. "You can't hit what you can't see."

Green Arrow was down to his last ball. With a mighty effort he threw his fastball through the air, and it soared right past her ear.

"Ha! You missed," shouted Silver Banshee, and she inhaled and prepared to scream.

THWACK!

The baseball bounced off a signpost, ricocheted off a tent pole, and crashed into her from behind, where she couldn't see it coming. She fell to the ground, alive but unconscious.

"Strike three!" called Green Arrow. "You're *out!*"

CHAPTER 16

Nightwing was moving cautiously through the dark and twisty hallways inside the House of Mirrors building. Hundreds of tall, dusty mirrors surrounded the hero on each wall, creating a long row of reflections. Suddenly the sinister voice of the Scarecrow filled the room.

"Welcome, Nightwing," he said. "You know, if my research has taught me anything, it's that there are *so* many possibilities."

Nightwing quietly withdrew an electrical baton and turned a corner. There in front of him were three giant mirrors reflecting his own image.

He stopped as the Scarecrow continued to speak. "And yet, in the end, it all comes down to us confronting ourselves."

Nightwing stared at his reflections and called out, "I'm not afraid of you!"

"Are you talking to me? Or the man in the mirror?" asked the Scarecrow.

Suddenly the villain's voice was very close. Nightwing smashed his reflection in one of the three mirrors, thinking Scarecrow might be behind it. As jagged pieces of glass fell to the ground, a thick, green smoke spewed out from behind the mirror and engulfed Nightwing.

"Uh-oh. Looks like seven years of bad luck for you," said the Scarecrow.

Nightwing stumbled backward, doubled over and coughing. He ran deeper into the maze of mirrors, down one hallway and then another. As he ran, the Scarecrow's voice filled the room.

"Let's go deeper, Nightwing," he called out. "When did it start? This need to stay in control. This discipline. As a child?"

Nightwing covered his ears, trying to shut out the Scarecrow's words. He fell into another room that was covered from floor to ceiling with four giant mirrors.

"Stop it!" he shouted.

Just then he heard something behind him. He turned to look at his reflection in one mirror, and saw with horror that he was a young boy again. He was Dick Grayson, the world-famous circus acrobat of the Flying Graysons aerial team.

"Childhood pressures, check," taunted the Scarecrow.

Nightwing turned away to look at another mirror. Now he saw the reflection of Robin the Teen Wonder, young partner to Batman, looking back at him.

"Adult responsibilities taken on at an early age, most likely," continued the Scarecrow.

Nightwing covered his eyes and screamed, "Enough! Make it stop!"

He then turned to the third mirror. He was dressed in his Nightwing outfit.

"Identity crisis, I'd wager," said the Scarecrow. "Because your nightmare is that you are becoming the thing you promised yourself you never would."

With a strangled cry Nightwing turned to the fourth mirror and saw an image of Batman reflected back at him.

Nightwing swung his baton and crashed through all four mirrors. The Scarecrow stepped through the broken glass and entered the room, carrying a razor-sharp scythe in his hands.

"I *will* stop it, I promise," he said. "Scarecrow will put an end to your pain."

The Scarecrow raised the scythe high above Nightwing and then brought it down with a savage speed.

CLANG!

The scythe bounced harmlessly off Nightwing's baton to the Scarecrow's surprise.

"What? But *how*?" sputtered the Scarecrow.

Nightwing spun the baton in his hand. "I conquered my fears at a very young age, Dr. Crane," Nightwing said as he used his baton to deflect the green globs of fear gas that Scarecrow was throwing at him.

Scarecrow turned and ran out of the room.

"What's the matter, Doctor? Is the Scarecrow running scared?" Nightwing asked.

The Scarecrow was breathing heavily as he ran down a mirrored corridor, and found himself at a dead end. But it wasn't the Scarecrow's reflection in the mirrors. He saw Nightwing, hundreds of Nightwings reflected back at him.

"Tell the truth, Scarecrow. This is *your* nightmare, isn't it?" said the real Nightwing.

WHAM!

Nightwing stepped forward and threw a powerful punch that knocked the Scarecrow off his feet. The villain sank to the ground and drifted into unconsciousness as Nightwing swiftly tied him up.

CHAPTER 17

Outside the fairgrounds warehouse, Solomon Grundy grunted angrily as Batman looped one more thick chain around the villain's body. The Dark Knight then attached a large, sturdy padlock to the chains.

Nearby, Silver Banshee was also tied up with ropes. Next to her was a giant glass canister that was tightly sealed, with Clayface inside.

A few feet away Red Robin was bandaging Gogo Shoto's wounds, and Green Arrow was busy assembling the components of a replacement bow.

"Back in the game, baby," he said happily as he held

his new bow aloft. It looked just like his old one.

Nightwing emerged from the House of Mirrors, dragging an unconscious Scarecrow.

"Got one more for you," Nightwing said, tossing a groaning Scarecrow at Batman's feet.

"Nice work," said Batman. "Put him with the rest."

Suddenly there was a rumbling sound in the distance. The heroes looked up.

"That'll be Mr. Giggles," said Green Arrow.

"Be ready for anything," cautioned Batman as he reached for a Batarang.

As the Joker's motorcycle roared into view, Nightwing grabbed two batons and started spinning them. Green Arrow readied a bow. Red Robin crouched into a fighting stance.

With a loud screech the Joker brought the motorcycle to a stop, and then hopped off the vehicle. He was wearing a tall cowboy hat, which he tipped to the four heroes.

"Well, lookee here," he drawled in a thick Southern accent. "Seems that a cowpoke can't even rustle up some supplies without the cavalry showing up!"

"We've taken down your team," Batman replied. "You can't beat us all by yourself, Joker."

"Oh, Batman," the Joker said. "You see, with my

virus I control the computers in your vehicles. And that means . . . I control your vehicles! So this showdown is not with *me*. It's with *them*!"

The Joker started laughing hysterically as he pointed to the end of the pier. Suddenly Cyborg, Ace the robotic wolf, the Batwing, and the Batmobile came into view, facing the heroes.

"Make 'em roadkill!" the Joker cried out happily as he activated a remote control device.

The Batwing soared through the air, its headlights glowing purple, and it fired two rocket blasts at the feet of the heroes.

BLAM! BLAM!

"Separate!" Batman yelled to the other heroes. "We need to divide and conquer. Red Robin, you need to get Gogo out of here."

Green Arrow fired an explosive arrow at the Batwing, but the machine swerved in the air to avoid the blast. It then changed course and flew directly toward Nightwing.

"I'm on it . . . I hope!" Nightwing called out as the Batwing zoomed closer. Just as it was about to collide with him, Nightwing hopped into the air, extended his baton, and landed on top of the flying Batwing.

Batman spun around just in time to see the Batmobile

bearing down on him, its headlights glowing an eerie purple. Batman crouched down, waiting until the vehicle was inches away from crashing into him. Then he flipped forward in the air, reached out to grab the vehicle, and drove the sharp cuffs of his gloves into the top of the car. The Batmobile swerved wildly, trying to loosen the Dark Knight's grip, but Batman held on.

Just then Ace leaped through the air, aiming for Green Arrow's throat. The hero ducked and quickly loaded an explosive arrow into his bow. Ace's mouth was opened wide, his razor-sharp metallic teeth glinting as he charged at Green Arrow.

BOOM!

The arrow soared into Ace's mouth and exploded. The cyber wolf collapsed to the ground, but seconds later it was back on its feet. Green Arrow fired a grapple arrow at the warehouse and soared up to the roof. Ace extended his claws and was soon climbing up the side of the warehouse in pursuit of Green Arrow.

Outside the warehouse the Joker was chuckling to himself as he cut Grundy's chains and then freed the other villains.

"Wake up, chuckleheads," the Joker said to them. "Let's get moving. Those toys won't keep them occupied forever. We still have a *world* to conquer!"

"Grundy feel like microwaved popcorn," he complained as he and the other villains hopped into their car.

At the far end of the pier, Red Robin removed an expanding hoverboard from his Utility Belt and handed it to Gogo. Cyborg could be seen in the distance, moving toward them.

"Take this hoverboard, and get gone," Red Robin said quickly.

"Freeze, Gogo Shoto!" commanded Cyborg.

"What about the cybernetic automaton yelling my name?" Gogo asked.

"I'll take care of him," replied Red Robin. "Meet me at the time and place I gave you. We could use your help."

"If I survive this," Gogo said nervously as he balanced atop the hoverboard. Then he zoomed out above the harbor.

Cyborg raised his wrist and pointed his white-noise cannon directly at Gogo, but Red Robin jumped up and knocked into Cyborg's arm before he could fire. Cyborg then pointed the cannon directly at Red Robin. A look of confusion came over Cyborg's face.

"I don't wanna . . . I don't wanna do this to you, man!"

he struggled to say. "But I must follow orders. . . ."

WHAM!

Cyborg fired his cannon, but Red Robin tumbled through the air to avoid the blast.

"You're shooting at me, Vic?" Red Robin yelled. "Here I thought we were friends!"

"I can't control it, man," Cyborg said in a pained voice. "The Joker virus is making me do it."

WHAM!

Cyborg fired again, but Red Robin used a baton to pole-vault over a nearby car and then started running down the pier. Cyborg popped his wings open and jetted after him.

High in the sky, Nightwing was still holding tight to the top of the Batwing. The machine banked to the right and left, and then it flipped 360 degrees. Still, Nightwing held on.

"You're not shaking me that easy," he called out.

Nightwing grabbed an electric baton and plunged it deep into a control box that was mounted behind the machine's cockpit.

ZZZZZZAP!

Sparks flew from the control box as the Batwing shuddered violently in the air. With all of its internal circuits destroyed, the Batwing started plummeting toward the harbor.

Seconds before the Batwing crashed into the water, Nightwing fired a grappling line from his baton. The line looped around a bridge and yanked him into the air. As the Batwing sank to the bottom of the harbor, Nightwing landed with a splash in the water.

"I never did enjoy surfing," he said as he spit the foul-tasting harbor water from his mouth.

CHAPTER 18

The sound of the Batmobile's screeching tires filled the streets of Gotham City. Batman crouched on top of the vehicle as it careened to the left and right. The car then crashed through a protective barrier and smashed into a construction site. Batman tumbled to the ground, and the Batmobile immediately turned around and started chasing him.

Batman tossed an exploding Batarang into the sky.

BLAM!

A highway overpass above him exploded from the impact, and large chunks of concrete fell onto the

Batmobile. The car was stuck under the debris.

Batman sighed in relief, and then he watched as the car's purple headlights glowed back to life in the rubble. The concrete chunks started shaking, and soon the Batmobile pushed its way loose. It was heading toward Batman again.

Thinking quickly, the Dark Knight ran into a nearby alley that he hoped would be too narrow for the Batmobile to follow him into.

The Batmobile slammed into the alleyway entrance, unable to reach Batman. As the car slowly backed up, twin panels at the front of the vehicle popped open, and two rocket launchers emerged. They were pointing right at Batman.

WHAM! WHAM!

Seconds before the rockets exploded within the alley, Batman fired a grappling line and soared high above the Batmobile. Before the car could turn around, Batman crouched on the ground, removed a manhole cover, and then jumped into the hole. Hanging on to a ladder, Batman grabbed his sharpest Batarang and waited for the Batmobile to return.

As the vehicle zoomed over the manhole, Batman reached up and sliced a hole in the Batmobile's fuel tank.

A thick stream of gas gushed from the car as it sped away down the street.

Seconds later the car screeched to a stop, turned around, and once again started speeding toward the open manhole. With a smile Batman struck a Batarang on the stream of gas, making it catch fire. Flames soon engulfed the Batmobile, causing the vehicle to swerve out of control. With a fiery explosion the Batmobile crashed into a building and finally came to a stop.

Back at the Gotham City fairgrounds, Green Arrow was rapidly climbing up the dilapidated wooden railings of the roller coaster, trying to avoid the angry cyber wolf that was just below him. Green Arrow then took a running leap and started sliding down the track of the roller coaster. He tumbled to the ground and began running through the fairgrounds. The robotic wolf was right behind him. Green Arrow turned a corner, only to discover that he was at a dead end. The metallic growl of the cyber wolf grew louder as it approached.

"Good doggie. Nice robot doggie," Green Arrow said soothingly as he drew two arrows from his quiver. He looked up and smiled as he noticed the rusty remnants of a rocket-ship amusement park ride dangling in the air above him.

The cyber wolf crouched and then pounced, zooming through the air toward Green Arrow.

Two arrows flew through the air and pierced the wires that were holding the rocket ship aloft.

CRASH!

The machine fell directly on top of the cyber wolf, which struggled for a few moments under the heavy load. Finally it stopped moving.

Green Arrow breathed a sigh of relief.

The explosive sounds of Cyborg's wrist cannon echoed through the empty streets of Gotham City. Red Robin was running for his life, trying to avoid the cannon blasts from his friend.

"You can beat this, Vic," Red Robin called out as he jumped on top of a parked car. "I know you can!"

Cyborg shook his head as he hovered in the air and responded, "I'm not responsible for my actions! There's *nothing* I can do to stop this!"

BLAM! BLAM! BLAM!

As Red Robin jumped from the top of one car to another, Cyborg blasted each automobile with his cannon.

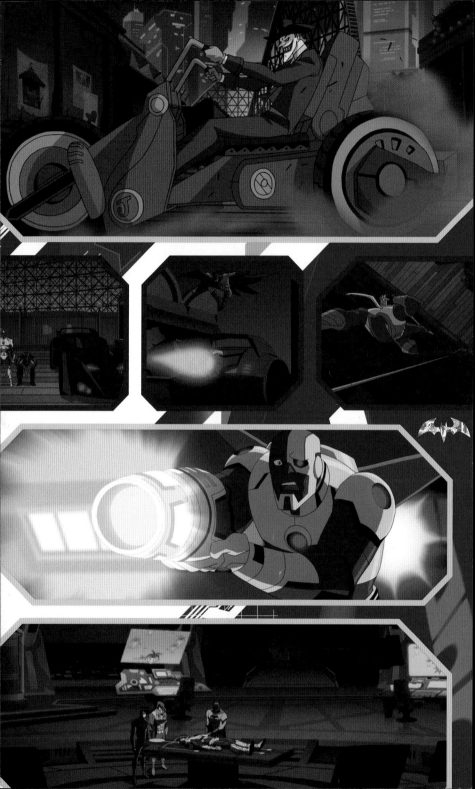

"I'm not leaving you, buddy," Red Robin yelled.

"Maybe we can help," called out Batman as he emerged on a nearby rooftop. Green Arrow and Nightwing stood beside him.

"You guys sure took your time showing up," Red Robin observed.

A look of pain washed over Cyborg's face as he turned his cannon toward the rooftop and said, "Now the Joker is going to make me stop you all!"

"No, he's not," Batman replied.

The Dark Knight quickly threw a Batarang that wedged into Cyborg's left wing jet. Cyborg was knocked off kilter and started spiraling down.

Just as Cyborg hit the ground, Green Arrow shot an arrow into a nearby water truck. The arrow knocked a hole in the side of the vehicle, and water started flooding into the street and splashing against Cyborg.

"Water won't stop me," Cyborg said with a laugh.

Nightwing reached for his electrical baton and hurled it toward Cyborg.

"Then how about this?" said Nightwing as his baton landed in the water.

Huge electrical sparks shot into the air and engulfed Cyborg. He fell to his knees and then collapsed on the ground. The electrical light in his eyes dimmed.

"Is he going to be okay?" Red Robin asked nervously.

"Get him to the cave," Batman said grimly. "This isn't over yet. The Joker is still out there."

CHAPTER 19

Usually, the cavernous television studio within the Gotham City news tower was swarming with activity as reporters, camera operators, and technicians prepared for the *Channel Six Evening News* broadcast. Now the Joker was sitting in the middle of the studio, smiling broadly as Grundy and Silver Banshee walked over to him.

"Sure, Batman took my hacker, and now Gogo is gone-gone," the Joker admitted. "But do you see *me* complaining? Nope! I've got my happy-pants on. Because it's time to send this baby worldwide. Why settle for Gotham City when we can rule the entire world?"

Suddenly the monitors in front of the Joker lit up and were filled with the leering face of the Joker avatar. A countdown clock appeared below the face, and it read 10:00:00.

"Mr. Joker," said the tinny voice of the avatar. "I'll be uploaded into the transmitter in only ten hours."

The Joker smiled with satisfaction. "Tonight, at the parade, we create Joker-World!" he yelled, and then jumped out of his chair, laughing hysterically. Soon he was surrounded by the other four villains, who joined in the laughter.

Then the monitor went dark.

Soon after, Commissioner Gordon was standing on the roof of Gotham City police headquarters, wearing the uniform of a first-year police officer. As he scanned the nearby buildings, Batman stepped out of the shadows behind him.

Gordon turned around and said, "I'm not supposed to be up here."

"I know," replied Batman.

Gordon sighed and said, "Grundy runs the police force like a kindergarten. We play games all day long to entertain Commissioner Grundy. The only reason I'm here at all is because I'm in the middle of a round of hide-and-seek with him."

"We're taking Joker down at the parade tonight. Be ready. We're going to need your help," said Batman.

"You've got it," said Gordon.

Batman disappeared into the shadows again.

Just then the door to the roof crashed open, and Grundy lumbered onto the roof.

"Found you!" Grundy yelled happily at Gordon.

"Yeah, I guess you did," muttered Gordon.

Far beneath Wayne Manor, Gogo Shoto stumbled down the steps leading to the Batcave as Red Robin held tightly to his arm. A blindfold covered Gogo's eyes.

"Almost there," Red Robin said. "Sorry about the blindfold, but we can't take any chances."

Gogo blinked when Red Robin removed the blindfold, and then he gasped when he realized that he was standing in the Batcave.

"Whoa! Look at this place! It's awesome," he said happily.

At a nearby workbench Batman leaned over the body of Cyborg and held a small, beeping mechanical device over his torso. There was no movement from Cyborg.

Nightwing and Green Arrow exchanged worried glances.

Gogo continued to walk through the Batcave, his mouth agape. He wandered over to the Batcomputer and saw that its screens were filled with multiple images of the Joker avatar.

"Do you mind?" Gogo asked as he sat down in front of the Batcomputer.

"Go ahead," replied Batman.

Red Robin stood behind Gogo and said to the young man, "Tell Batman what you told me."

Without looking up as he continued to work on the computer, Gogo said, "The Joker's got an artificial intelligence to deliver the digital laughter virus he had me build."

"Can you hack the AI?" asked Batman, wondering if the system could be hacked remotely.

"No, it's a closed system. But I can build you an interface to *physically* hack the AI if you can find the hard drive containing it."

"But we don't know where that is," said Green Arrow.

Suddenly the computer screen lit up with another Joker dispatch. This time the Joker was reading from a stack of notes and sitting behind the Channel Six Evening News desk.

"This is Joker with your news flash," he said, pretending to be a newscaster. "Gotham City prepares for tonight's parade in honor of their beloved King Joker!"

"What's the forecast for this evening, Joker?" the Joker asked, now dressed as a female news anchor.

"I can turn this off," Gogo said as he reached for the keyboard.

"Hold on," said Batman. "That broadcast is coming from the Channel Six studio."

On-screen the Joker was now standing in front of a weather chart, in yet another outfit, to deliver the weather report.

"Looks good, Joker," he declared. "As long as we can keep the evening free of horrible flying rodents, everything will be fantastic!"

Batman stared at the screen and then said, "Computer, magnify and search!"

The Batcomputer screen froze on the image of the Joker and then zoomed in to locate a small video display unit at the back of the room. As the computer zoomed in even closer, the letters *AI* could be seen on the screen.

"The AI is in the control room mainframe," Batman said. "Joker is going to try to send this virus worldwide. We need to stop him."

Gogo reached into his pocket and extracted a virtual-reality mask, then said to Batman, "With the interface, you're going to need something else to get into the AI world."

Gogo handed Batman the mask.

CHAPTER 20

The sounds of marching bands and an out-of-tune circus calliope echoed through the streets of downtown Gotham City. The sidewalks were filled with unhappy citizens, their faces covered with garish Joker masks. Frightened children huddled close to their parents, who watched with dismay as a giant Joker float rumbled down the street.

A float for the Gotham City Police Department was the next to arrive. At the front of the float was a giant bust of Solomon Grundy's head, a police cap perched atop the grotesque head. At the back of the float, Grundy himself was sitting on a giant throne, surrounded by James Gordon and a group of other police officers.

Grundy glared at the buildings as the float passed down the street, and he said, "Be on the lookout for Batman and friends. If you see him, tell me, and I'll use *this!*"

Gordon's eyes widened as Grundy lifted a giant rocket launcher in his arms and pointed it in the air.

Silver Banshee stood on top of the next float, and she cleared her throat before singing a few notes, "La! La! La!"

Scarecrow and Clayface followed on the last two floats. Scarecrow snarled at the crowds, which shrank back from him in fear. Clayface raised his two massive arms triumphantly in the air, only to receive a tiny smattering of applause from the confused citizens.

On the Gotham City police float, Gordon suddenly had an idea.

"Look! There's Batman!" he called out as he pointed to a nearby rooftop.

"What? Where?" barked Grundy, and he pointed the rocket launcher and fired.

BLAM!

The rocket flew into the air and then burst like a firework.

"My mistake," Gordon said. "I thought I saw something."

Another police officer realized what Gordon was doing, and she called out, "There he is!"

BLAM!

Grundy fired again. There was another firework. The crowds oohed and aahed.

"No, no. Over there!" said another cop.

BLAM! BLAM! BLAM!

CLICK!

Grundy pulled the trigger again, but nothing happened.

"Grundy out of ammo," he said. "Grundy reload."

As Grundy reached down to grab more rockets, Gordon pulled a small remote control device from his pocket and pressed a button. A trapdoor opened up on the float, and Grundy tumbled down into a secret compartment. Seconds later six thick metal clamps encircled his wrists, chest, and ankles, pinning him to a table.

"No! I boss!" he bellowed as Gordon slammed the trapdoor shut, leaving Grundy in the dark.

Across town in the television studio inside the Gotham City news tower, the Joker was tapping his fingers impatiently on the news desk and staring at a large video screen. The face of the smiling Joker avatar filled the screen, and below it a digital clock counted down. It now read 00:12:36.

"C'mon, c'mon. Over twelve minutes to go," the Joker said with disgust. "It's like Christmas morning, except I'm waiting for world domination!"

The Joker was so focused on the countdown clock that he didn't hear Batman silently dropping down to the floor behind him. Moving into the shadows, Batman moved to the AI video panel. The Dark Knight punched a series of buttons below the panel, and a screen message appeared: "AI Online: Link-Up Complete."

Batman then placed Gogo's virtual-reality mask over his cowl. The mask lit up, and suddenly Batman found himself standing in the middle of a barren desert, with nothing but sand and golden skies surrounding him. Batman was now a digital character within the Joker's world of virtual reality. As Batman scanned the horizon, a chilling laugh could be heard behind him. Batman spun around and saw that a digital version of the Joker was suddenly standing next to him.

"I was wondering when you'd show up," the Joker said.

Batman quickly reached out to grab the Joker, but the villain disappeared. The virtual Joker then materialized ten feet away.

"It's not going to be that easy," he said, shaking his head with disgust. "You're in *my* world now. And I like things a little . . . *crazy!*"

Batman looked down at his hands and watched with dismay as his fingers started expanding. Soon they were twice the normal size, then three times as large. His arms and chest and stomach grew, and then his legs started expanding. Soon he was almost as round as a balloon.

"I can do whatever I want here," the Joker said as he doubled over in laughter. "If I dream it, it's true. I can make you Fatman! Run, Fatman, run!"

Suddenly twelve identical Jokers appeared in a row. The virtual Batman stumbled back a few steps, and then he felt himself compelled to run away from the Jokers.

"This . . . is . . . not . . . real," wheezed the virtual Batman as he lumbered across the desert sands.

"It's as real as you are, amigo!" the Jokers cried out as they gave chase.

The virtual Batman was panting heavily as he ran.

Up ahead was the edge of a steep cliff above a canyon. Batman looked behind him and saw that the Jokers were closing in on him. There was only one thing to do. Batman accelerated his pace, took a flying leap, and dove over the edge of the cliff.

The Jokers were not only right behind him, but they had transformed into deadly pterodactyls, howling with delight as they pursued Batman.

"Two can play this game," Batman said grimly as he plummeted toward the floor of the canyon. Using all his willpower, he suddenly transformed back to his normal size and reached out to extend his cape. With a snap his cape transformed into glider wings, allowing Batman to sail safely to the ground.

CRUNCH!

One of the pterodactyls lunged for Batman, its mouth open wide and its sharp teeth glinting in the desert sunlight.

Batman dodged the deadly beast and then spun around to see the other twelve creatures heading right for him.

Batman stood his ground and, concentrating with all his might, created a giant virtual *Tyrannosaurus rex* robot. Batman climbed on top of the cyber creature, and soon his robot was charging toward the startled pterodactyls.

Batman then reached down to touch a panel on the robot, which sprung open to reveal a formidable laser cannon. Batman pointed the cannon toward the ptero- dactyls and started firing.

BLAM! BLAM! BLAM!

After each pterodactyl exploded in the sky, the parts fell to the ground and were replaced by five more digital Jokers. Soon Batman was surrounded by several dozen laughing Jokers. He hopped off the cyber dinosaur and faced the Jokers.

One of the Jokers stepped forward and said, "It looks like your amazing *B. rex* has made more of me instead of less! You can't win. You can't beat me in my own game, Batman. Game over!"

The Dark Knight smiled in response as his right glove began to emit a soft blue light, and a woman's comput- erized voice announced, "Upload complete." At the same time a giant, glowing blue Batarang materialized at the end of the cyber dinosaur's metallic tail.

The Joker looked puzzled and asked, "What's going on now? Who was that? She sounds lovely."

With a snarl the Joker then lunged forward and charged at Batman, throwing a wild punch. Batman easily caught the Joker's hand in his own and grasped it tightly. The soft blue light extended from Batman's right glove and illuminated the Joker's arm.

POP!

The virtual Joker was transformed into a virtual Batman. The two Dark Knights faced each other. The other virtual Jokers watched in alarm as the cyber dinosaur emitted a loud roar and charged toward them.

SMASH! BLAM! CRASH!

The glowing blue tail of the robotic *T. rex* slammed into a dozen virtual Jokers, instantly transforming them into a dozen Dark Knights. Each Batman slugged a Joker, which transformed into another Batman. Soon the desert was filled with dozens of virtual Dark Knights and only one Joker.

"Oof!" cried the Joker as Batman grabbed the villain and held him in place.

"Looks like your virus caught a virus," Batman said grimly.

"Come on!" the Joker wailed. "That's cheating!"

Back at the Joker parade, Silver Banshee was standing on top of her float, gesturing dramatically and singing a tuneless melody.

Suddenly a man standing on the sidewalk started yelling, "Boo!"

It was Green Arrow, but he had covered his face with a hat, scarf, and heavy overcoat to avoid being seen.

Then Silver Banshee sang a loud, off-key note that shattered all the glass in a nearby shop window.

More boos came from the crowds on the sidewalk, and various people called out to Banshee, "You're terrible!" and "Quit it!"

"Stop it, all of you!" she yelled.

Silver Banshee was so angry that she didn't even hear the soft thump as Green Arrow landed on her float.

WHOOOOOSH!

Silver Banshee turned just as one of Green Arrow's knockout-gas arrows exploded in her face.

The crowd burst into cheers as Silver Banshee toppled back onto the float.

Not far behind, the Scarecrow craned his neck to see what the commotion was about. As he reached into his pocket to grab a fear bomb, Nightwing swung through the air and silently landed behind him. Nightwing then reached forward and touched the Scarecrow's shoulder.

"Boo!" he said.

The Scarecrow jumped back in fright, but he quickly

regained his composure and prepared to toss his fear bomb.

"Not this time, Doctor," said Nightwing as he grabbed his baton and slammed it against the Scarecrow.

Scarecrow swayed on his feet for a few seconds, and then he crumpled to the floor of the float.

From the next float Clayface could see what had happened to the Scarecrow. With a roar Clayface raised himself to his full height and prepared to go after Nightwing.

Just as the monster stretched out his giant paw, Red Robin landed on top of the float and confronted Clayface. The young hero started flinging small, marble-size globes into Clayface's chest.

Clayface smiled as the globes oozed harmlessly into his body.

"Your explosives can't harm me," he said with a laugh.

"Explosives?" said Red Robin. "No, those were fast-hardening powdered cement pellets."

Clayface frowned and said, "Wait, what? I'll crush you!"

Clayface smacked his fists together and began charging toward Red Robin. Then he groaned and started moving more slowly. One arm froze midpunch, and the other came to a stop inches away from Red Robin's throat. Clayface strained to stretch his fingers, but they were no longer moving. The monster was frozen in position on the float.

"Whew! So close," Red Robin said with relief.

The floats came to a stop. As the heroes dragged the four villains from their floats, the crowds on the sidewalks erupted in cheers.

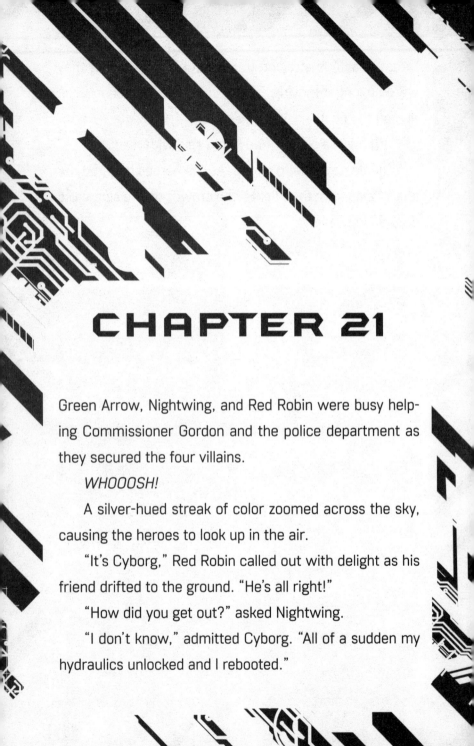

CHAPTER 21

Green Arrow, Nightwing, and Red Robin were busy help-ing Commissioner Gordon and the police department as they secured the four villains.

WHOOOSH!

A silver-hued streak of color zoomed across the sky, causing the heroes to look up in the air.

"It's Cyborg," Red Robin called out with delight as his friend drifted to the ground. "He's all right!"

"How did you get out?" asked Nightwing.

"I don't know," admitted Cyborg. "All of a sudden my hydraulics unlocked and I rebooted."

"That's great," said Red Robin.

"No, it's not," Cyborg said fiercely as his bionic eye suddenly started glowing with a dark purple hue. "I'm trying to fight it, but my programming won't let me!"

BLAM!

Cyborg fired a laser blast from his wrist cannon that almost hit Red Robin.

"He's still being controlled! Look out!" yelled Green Arrow.

Green Arrow, Red Robin, and Nightwing ran to take cover as Cyborg blasted his friends.

Nightwing somersaulted to the ground and then launched an electrical baton at Cyborg. It lodged in the middle of his chest panel, causing him to stagger backward. Then Cyborg ripped the baton from his chest and threw it directly at Nightwing. The hero flew through the air.

Red Robin snuck up behind Cyborg and swung his staff. *CRASH!* It collided with Cyborg's head, causing him to drop to the ground in pain.

"Cyborg, stop," pleaded Red Robin. "You have to fight this. You're more than a machine!"

Cyborg staggered to his feet and said, "I can't. Get clear before I . . ."

Without finishing his sentence, Cyborg kicked Red Robin in the chest, sending him crashing against a wall.

POP! POP! POP!

Three explosive arrows detonated across Cyborg's chest. Green Arrow stepped forward, pointing two more arrows directly at his friend.

"Sorry to do this, buddy, but I can't let the Joker win," said Green Arrow.

Cyborg marched forward, his bionic eye glowing purple. He reached forward to knock Green Arrow's bow and arrows to the ground. He grabbed the archer's neck and lifted him into the air.

"The Joker already *has* won," Cyborg said grimly.

Back in the Joker's world of artificial intelligence, dozens of virtual Dark Knights were chasing the one remaining Joker. Each time a Batman swung, the Joker ducked. The villain looked at the digital countdown timer on his wristwatch. Twenty seconds.

BLAM!

While the Joker had been checking his watch, he'd collided headfirst with the cyber dinosaur. The Joker sailed through the air and landed with a crash against a desert rock. He looked at his watch again and saw that there were only ten seconds left on the clock.

"Too late, Batman," he said with a laugh. "You've run out of . . . What the . . ."

The virtual Joker looked down at his feet and watched in horror as his shoes started transforming into Batman's boots. Soon his entire lower torso was a duplicate of Batman's. His countdown clock read five . . . four . . .

"No! Quit it!" the Joker screamed as he swatted at his legs. "Betrayed by my own legs. What a way to go!"

The digital transformation was almost complete. A bat-symbol appeared on his chest. Soon his leering face was replaced by Batman's cowl.

He sank to the ground and said, "Well, at least I went doing what I loved—mocking you!"

Inside the Gotham City news tower, the real Joker was staring intently at the countdown clock on the screen in front of him.

"Three . . . two . . . one . . . zero!" As he pushed a giant red button, he yelled with delight, "Bye-bye, boring world. Hello, new fun Joker-World!"

There was silence. The Joker frowned and pushed the button again.

"Why isn't anything happening?" the Joker screamed

while he pounded his fist against the button.

When the word *Malfunction* appeared on the screen, the Joker spun around just as Batman stepped out of the shadows.

"You! You've ruined everything!" the Joker yelled as the video screens around him went dark.

The Joker jumped out of his chair and then tossed the chair across the room. Batman jumped out of the way, and the Joker ran to the elevator door, pulled it open, and then leaped into the empty elevator chute.

"I've still got a couple tricks up my sleeve, Bats," the Joker cried out as he tumbled down the elevator shaft, throwing three small Joker bombs into the air. As they exploded next to Batman, the Joker disappeared into the darkness.

Batman peered into the elevator shaft, but there was no sign of the Joker.

On the street below the Gotham City news tower, Cyborg was still clutching Green Arrow's throat in his mechanical fist. As the lights flickered in the building above them, the purple glowing light in Cyborg's bionic eye began to fade. He loosened his grip, and Green Arrow tumbled to the ground, gasping for breath.

"What's going on?" asked Red Robin.

"I think we won," replied Nightwing. "Everything is rebooting."

All around the heroes the streetlights began to glow, and the video screens on top of the building hummed to life again. The nervous pedestrians that were huddling on the sidewalks began to cheer.

Red Robin placed his hand on Cyborg's shoulder and said, "Welcome back, big guy. How do you feel?"

"Like I'll be cleaning my hard drive for a week," he said groggily.

Suddenly all of the lights in the city switched off again. Only the giant video screens in downtown Gotham City were shining, and each one featured the leering face of the Joker.

"Hiya, sports fans!" he called out. "You didn't really think that I would transmit my digital laughter virus from only *one* location, did you? *Suckers!*"

The Joker's face disappeared, and the screen then began flashing a new countdown clock, this time with only ten minutes on it.

Batman swung to the street at the end of a Batrope.

"The Joker's got another transmitter," said Nightwing.

"We've got to find it. Fast!" said Batman.

The Joker's face suddenly reappeared on the screen as he taunted, "But, just to keep you occupied in the meantime . . ."

BLAM!

The crowds started screaming as a giant mechanical Joker robot, more than fifty feet tall, crashed through the brick facade of the Gotham City news tower. It slammed a giant metal fist into the side of the building, sending a pile of bricks tumbling to the ground. Batman and Red Robin quickly pushed a group of terrified pedestrians to safety.

"This day keeps getting better," said Green Arrow as he shot a net arrow into the air to prevent more building debris from falling to the ground.

"We're going to need tech to take that thing down," said Nightwing.

"What gear do you suggest? Everything is powered off again," said Red Robin.

Batman turned to the heroes and said, "Cyborg, keep him busy. The rest of you, follow me. I know where we can get some reliable equipment."

"Ha! Ha! Ha!" boomed the mechanical voice of the Joker robot as it rampaged through the streets of Gotham City, crushing automobiles beneath its giant feet. Crowds of people were screaming in fear as they ran from the machine.

Cyborg launched himself into the air, flying past a video screen that now had a countdown clock with six minutes left on it.

"Joke's over, Joker!" Cyborg called out as he fired one laser blast after another at the robot.

The Joker robot laughed in response and easily lifted a car off the street. The deadly machine threw the auto directly toward Cyborg, knocking the hero to the ground.

The real Joker, sitting at a control panel inside the robot, reached for a microphone and said, "Is that all you've got, Batman? One Tin Man? This'll be easier than I dreamed!"

ZOOOM!

"Wait . . . what's that?" the Joker asked as he peered into the sky above him.

The loud roar of a World War II fighter plane filled the air as it dove toward the Joker robot. Batman was piloting the plane, and he grabbed a lever to fire at the robot.

"Nightwing, Red Robin, you're up next," Batman said into his communicator.

"What's going on?" the Joker demanded as he spun the robot in circles, trying to avoid the vintage plane's machine-gun fire. "Is this an antiques show?"

VROOOM!

Two 1950s motorcycles then sped into view, with Nightwing and Red Robin atop the vehicles. The heroes quickly circled around the Joker robot, which staggered to the left and right, unsure which way to proceed.

"I never thought I'd say this," said Red Robin into his communicator, "but thank goodness for the history museum!"

The Joker robot slammed its giant fists into the streets, trying to dislodge both heroes, but they easily avoided the robot's blows.

Nightwing and Red Robin then halted their vehicles, one on each side of the Joker robot. Both heroes launched plastic explosives into the air. The Joker watched in dismay as they landed on top of his robot.

WHAM!

The top of the robot cracked open, revealing the Joker sitting in the driver's seat, frantically pulling levers and trying to turn the robot around.

"Come on, you hunk of junk!" he yelled. And then he looked up to say, "Uh-oh."

A dark green World War II–era tank had rumbled into view and was moving toward him. Inside the tank, Green

Arrow peered into a periscope and took aim at the Joker robot.

BLAM!

The entire street shook as the Joker robot was shattered into tiny pieces. Flames and thick black smoke drifted from the wreckage.

As the heroes moved closer, a figure stepped out of the billowing smoke. It was the Joker, and he was wearing a Kevlar suit of armor. On his back was a flight pack. Seconds later he fired up the rocket blasters on his flight pack and was levitating in the air.

"Gotta fly, spoilsports," the Joker yelled as he looked at the digital countdown clock on the screen. "See you in three minutes . . . when I rule the world!"

The Joker zoomed into the sky above downtown Gotham City, soaring through the air and laughing wildly. A minute later he looked back to see the vintage airplane in pursuit. Batman was firing at the Joker.

"Like the suit? It's new!" called out the Joker as he swerved in the air.

Batman reached for his communicator and said, "Gogo, are there any other transmitters powerful enough to upload this virus worldwide?"

Inside the Batcave, Gogo was working at the

Batcomputer, and he replied, "Not that I can find, Batman. The Joker would need a quantum computer. Or maybe even a *boosted* quantum computer."

ZAP! ZAP!

The Joker had extended his wrists toward Batman's plane and fired at the Dark Knight.

"Got your back!" called out Cyborg as he zoomed into view next to the plane and fired two laser blasts from his wrist cannons to destroy the weapons. Cyborg then rocketed past Batman's plane, in pursuit of the Joker.

"Less than one minute on the countdown clock," said the voice of Nightwing on Batman's communicator.

"Wait, I've got it," Batman said into his communicator. "*Cyborg* is the transmitter!"

"I'm the *what* now?" asked Cyborg with surprise.

"That's why your systems unlocked before I beat the AI," said Batman. "The Joker must have the gem attached to you somehow."

Cyborg continued to pursue the Joker as his bionic eye did a digital scan of his interior machinery. He scanned his right arm and found nothing. Then he looked inside his left arm. There, buried within his mechanical forearm, was the Inca energy gem. Below it a digital countdown clock said there were twenty-seven seconds left.

"You're right, it's here. Do I just yank it out or what?" asked Cyborg.

Gogo was studying a schematic diagram on the Batcomputer and replied, "No! You could trigger the virus. You're going to have to connect the gem to the Joker's suit. The feedback should shut everything down."

Cyborg fired a rocket thruster and zoomed through the air in pursuit of the Joker.

"Can't catch me. I'm the gingerbread man!" yelled the Joker as Cyborg flew closer.

"Where do I attach this thing?" Cyborg called out to Gogo.

"I don't know," Gogo said, "but attach it to the wrong place, and it's Joker-World forever!"

Green Arrow's voice then announced, "And you only have fifteen seconds."

"Great, no pressure," said Cyborg.

As Cyborg and the plane flew closer to the Joker, Batman tapped his cowl, activating a digital screen that analyzed the Joker's flight suit.

"The Joker's suit is stolen military tech that was built by Wayne Enterprises," he reported. "The AI must have found it when it hacked Gotham City. Cyborg, I'm uploading the specs to your subnet. Good luck."

Cyborg poured on the speed, flying directly behind the Joker. Cyborg extended his mechanical arm until his hand wrapped around the Joker's ankle. He pulled himself closer to the Joker and landed on top of the villain's back. The digital clock in Cyborg's arm told him he had five seconds.

"Get off me, you metallic bully!" the Joker cried out.

Cyborg quickly studied the specs for the Joker's flight suit with his bionic eye, and zeroed in on the area between the Joker's shoulders.

"That should be where the central core is," Cyborg said nervously as he reached forward with his right hand. There were three seconds left on the clock.

"Here goes everything," said Cyborg as he punched his left fist into the Joker's flight suit. Then he pushed forward so that his forearm reached within the interior of the suit.

KA-BOOM!

The Joker's suit exploded into flames, and Cyborg was knocked back by the impact. As Cyborg reeled through the air, the Joker plummeted into Gotham Harbor and sank beneath the murky waters.

Cyborg hovered over the harbor, scanning the water with his bionic eye. There was no sign of the Joker.

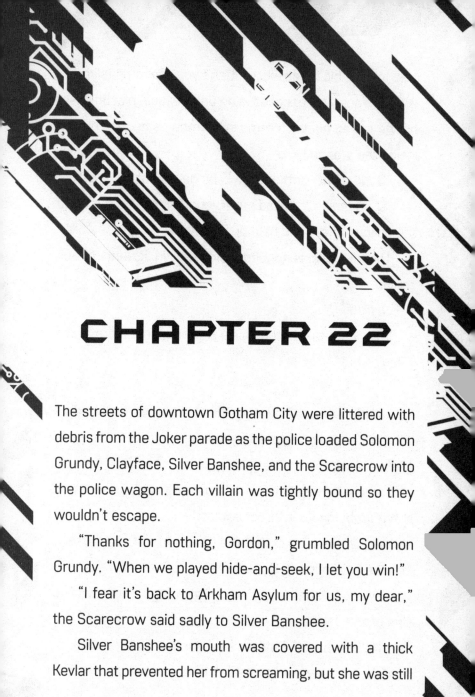

CHAPTER 22

The streets of downtown Gotham City were littered with debris from the Joker parade as the police loaded Solomon Grundy, Clayface, Silver Banshee, and the Scarecrow into the police wagon. Each villain was tightly bound so they wouldn't escape.

"Thanks for nothing, Gordon," grumbled Solomon Grundy. "When we played hide-and-seek, I let you win!"

"I fear it's back to Arkham Asylum for us, my dear," the Scarecrow said sadly to Silver Banshee.

Silver Banshee's mouth was covered with a thick Kevlar that prevented her from screaming, but she was still able to mumble in response, "Don't you *ever* stop talking?"

Clayface was encased in an unbreakable plastic case, but he raised his thick arms in triumph as he was placed inside the wagon.

"Good night, Gotham City!" he called out.

"Quick selfie?" called out a young boy as he ran up to the police wagon and held up his phone.

The four villains nodded their heads in agreement and smiled.

CLICK!

The photo taken, the police slammed the doors of the vehicle shut.

From atop a nearby building the five heroes watched as the police wagon moved out, beginning its journey to Arkham Asylum.

Cyborg turned to Green Arrow and said, "Hey, sorry about grabbing your throat earlier."

"No worries. Hazard of the job," replied Green Arrow. "You've got an iron grip, though."

"We combed the bay," said Nightwing. "There was no sign of the Joker."

"He'll be back," Batman said grimly.

"We'll be here when he is," said Green Arrow. "I can

always count on Gotham City for a thrill. See you around, Bats."

Green Arrow fired a grapple arrow into a nearby building and swung through the air, disappearing from view. Cyborg and Nightwing then sailed over the edge of the roof.

"I should start rebuilding the car," announced Red Robin as he fired a Batarang and launched himself into the air.

Batman stood alone on the rooftop, surveying Gotham Bay in the distance. He frowned and then melted into the shadows.

A full moon was shining above Gotham Bay. On the far shore, opposite Gotham City, a lonely figure struggled out of the dark water, shivering in the cold night air and squishing as he walked through the marshy grass. It was the Joker.

"Stupid plan. *Should* have worked," he muttered angrily. "I should be king of the world right now!"

The Joker paused for a moment, reached into his pants, and pulled out a struggling fish. The Joker giggled as he tossed the fish back into the water.

"Oh well, better luck next time," he said as he trudged

down a deserted country road. "Maybe I'll open up a toy store. Or a pizza joint! Oooh, I could open up a restaurant chain and call it Giggles! I like the sound of that!"

As he trudged deeper into the woods, the maniacal sound of his laughter filled the sky.

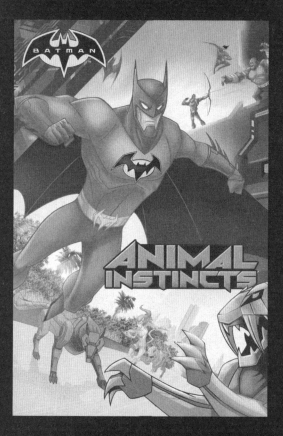

The sky over Gotham City was growing darker as night approached. Businesspeople left their office buildings and flooded into the subway stations, eager to get home from work. Others darted between stores, finishing up the last of their shopping before the evening rush was in full swing. Still, they all knew to stay as far as possible from the dimly lit alleys where criminals often lurked. Even the members of the Gotham City Police Department walked cautiously through the city's streets after the sun went down.

Despite the best efforts of the police, Gotham City's

criminals were always finding new ways to outsmart the law. Police hovercrafts floated above the buildings. Occasionally, a bright spotlight would shine from above, illuminating the inky black streets below in search of trouble.

Skyscrapers towered high above the bustling streets of downtown Gotham City, and along those buildings were dozens of bright neon signs and video screens. The largest video screen was almost fifty feet tall and covered the side of a building. The evening news was being broadcast on that screen, and a young newscaster smiled with excitement as she spoke. Behind her was an animated image of a giant asteroid flying through outer space.

"There are just three more days until Gotham City will be able to spot the passage of Midas Heart, the asteroid with a solid gold core that passes the Earth every seventy-seven years," she said.

The screen then switched to an image of an unusual-looking man who was wearing a tuxedo and an old-fashioned top hat. He had a long, sharp nose and wore a monocle in his right eye.

The newscaster continued, "And finally, tonight is the grand opening of the Aviary, Gotham City's newest and tallest building. Count on high society to flock to Oswald Cobblepot's *very* exclusive opening-night celebration."

A police hovercraft floated quietly past the video screen. Inside the craft, two policemen were dressed in combat gear. The dispatcher from police headquarters came over the radio as they piloted the craft higher.

"Go ahead, four-oh-nine. What's your status?"

"All clear from up here, dispatch," one of the policemen said. "Re-engaging for another pass."

The dispatcher's voice crackled over the communicator in response. "Roger that, four-oh-nine." There was a pause, and then she spoke in almost a whisper. "Hey, Tony . . . have you seen him tonight?"

"Sorry, buddy, not tonight," the policeman said as he peered through the windows of the hovercraft. "No sign of the Batman."

"All right. Let me know if you do, huh?" she said.

As the hovercraft glided over the skyline, a dark figure moved within the shadows atop one building. The figure waited until the police vehicle was out of sight, and then he stepped forward into the moonlight. It was Batman, the masked crime fighter who prowled the streets and rooftops of Gotham City in search of criminals. During the day, Batman was secretly Bruce Wayne, CEO of Wayne Enterprises and one of the world's wealthiest men. In the evening, he became Batman, the Dark Knight of Gotham City. He was not only a skilled fighter, but also a master detective.

Batman moved to the ledge of the building and fired his grapple launcher.

WHOOSH!

A long metal cord with a sharp hook at the end shot out of the device. The hook lodged itself into a nearby building, and within seconds Batman was swinging through the air, his fist holding tightly on to the cord and his black cape flowing behind him.

Just as Batman was about to crash into the next building over, he released his hand from the cord and extended his cape into two flexible glider wings, allowing him to sail silently through the air. As he soared high above Gotham, he scanned the city streets below for any signs of trouble.

PING!

Batman received an electronic alert on the communicator device on his cowl. It was Alfred, the trusted butler of Bruce Wayne. Alfred also served as one of Batman's most devoted assistants.

"Yes, Alfred?" asked Batman.

"I had a question that simply could not wait, sir," said Alfred.

Batman effortlessly flew over the building rooftops, remaining in the shadows as much as possible and avoiding the glare of the bright neon lights and video screens below.

"Which is?" he said, urging Alfred to continue.

Alfred replied, "I was inquiring as to which suit Bruce Wayne might need pressed for his meetings tomorrow."

Batman reached up to his cowl and tapped the area next to his right eye. With each tap, the lenses in his mask shifted from night vision to infrared to X-ray, allowing him to better scan the dark streets below.

"*That* was your question that couldn't wait?" Batman asked gruffly.

"These are the things that keep me up at night, Master Bruce," Alfred replied calmly.

Batman smiled as he adjusted his wings and banked high into the air.

"Was there anything else, Alfred?" Batman asked.

"I was inquiring how much longer your patrol would go on this evening. You see, I've cooked coq au vin." Alfred sighed.

There was a long pause as Batman adjusted his scanners. Something was going on at S.T.A.R. Labs, the laboratory complex downtown.

"Looks like I'll be late. I've got work to do," said Batman as he shifted position and started his descent toward the center of Gotham City.

Looking for another great book?
Find it
IN THE MIDDLE.

Fun, fantastic books for kids
in the in-beTWEEN age.

IntheMiddleBooks.com